To Jacob and Alex, creators of Taurs

First published in the UK in 2008 by Scholastic Children's Books
An imprint of Scholastic Ltd
Euston House, 24 Eversholt Street
London, NW1 1DB, UK
Registered office: Westfield Road, Southam, Warwickshire, CV47 0RA
SCHOLASTIC and associated logos are trademarks and or registered trademarks of Scholastic Inc.

Text copyright © Ali Sparkes, 2008
Illustration copyright © Dynamo Design, 2008

The right of Ali Sparkes and Dynamo Design to be identified as the author
and illustrator of this work has been asserted by them.

Cover illustration © Dynamo Design, 2008

ISBN 978 1 407 10292 4

A CIP catalogue record for this book
is available from the British Library

Printed by CPI Bookmarque, Croydon, CR0 4TD
Papers used by Scholastic Children's Books are made from wood grown in
sustainable forests.

1 3 5 7 9 10 8 6 4 2

This is a work of fiction. Names, characters, places,
incidents and dialogues are products of the author's imagination
or are used fictitiously. Any resemblance to actual people,
living or dead, events or locales is entirely coincidental.

www.scholastic.co.uk/zone
www.alisparkes.com

Chapter One

Head Banging

Lewis hung upside down by one foot, his ankle hopelessly stuck in a prickly branch, high up in the Screaming Tree of Torment.

"Help! Jack! Henry! Kevin! HELP ME! Quick! Before it starts screaming!" he bawled, as last month's pocket money began to fall out of his trousers and rain past his face in a stream of copper and silver.

Hanging upside down was bad enough, and Lewis thought his head might explode if he was stuck here much longer – but the tree hadn't started screaming yet and when it did... oh... when it did...

Well, it wasn't called the Screaming Tree of Torment for nothing.

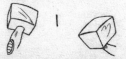

"We're coming! Hang on!" bellowed Jack, tiptoeing along as quickly as he could. His arms were outstretched and waggling as if he was walking a tightrope – so were Kevin and Henry's arms. They couldn't run to save Jack's little brother. They were in the middle of the Candyfloss Fields of Doom and a single wrong step could snag a tripwire attached to one of the sweet-smelling candyfloss plants and that would shake open a nest of Insectomites, which would swarm all over them and sting them into a pulp.

"I don't think I can hang on much longer," whimpered Lewis. "My eyeballs are going to pop!"

"Don't give up!" yelled Jack. "We'll save you!"

Just then the whole tree, from roots to trunk to branches to twigs, began to vibrate. Lewis yelped and clapped his hands over his upside-down ears. But it would do no good. The Screaming Tree of Torment was getting ready to scream.

"Go back!" he shrieked. "It's too late! Go back! Save yourselves!"

2

The tree began to whine and then the whine built to a loud whinge and then, in an awful punch of noise that bashed into everyone's ears like two lumps of concrete, it began to scream. And scream. And SCREAM. The sound of a thousand fingernails scraping against a thousand chalkboards, combined with five hundred electric saws going through five hundred sheets of iron, topped off with the squeal of twenty-five angry babies, filled the air.

Lewis, Jack, Henry and Kevin all joined in with the screaming, and clapped their hands to their ears, trying to block out the sound but it was no good.

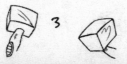

3

Four seconds later all their heads exploded.

"Jack, Lewis, Kevin, Henry – please get up and go and wash your hands," said Miss White. "You should be queuing up for lunch now, not dying agonizing deaths all over the tarmac."

"But our heads have just exploded," pointed out Jack.

"It's SATs week," said Miss White. "I'm not a bit surprised. My own is booked to explode at 3.15 this afternoon. I'd steer clear of the staffroom if I were you."

They all got up and dusted themselves off. Lewis shook his head a few times. He'd been dangling backwards over the low playground wall for quite a few minutes and really had felt that his eyeballs *might* pop.

"Let's play Screaming Tree and Candyfloss Fields of Doom again tomorrow," said Kevin. "And next time *I'll* be up the tree. And Grippakillataur could be chasing you guys too and Lightningtaur can come and save you."

"Not Lightningtaur, you noob!" said Jack. "Electrotaur."

They washed their hands and then joined the untidy queue for lunch.

"I like playing Tauronia games," said Henry to Lewis. He and Lewis, at seven, were in the same class, while Jack and Kevin were in the same class two years above. Year threes and year fives would never normally play together, but the Tauronia games were so good that Kevin and Jack were sometimes willing to hang out with the younger kids to play them. Lewis, like Jack, had a fantastic imagination and his games usually had a whole gang of boys wanting to join in.

Lewis felt slightly uneasy. He moved closer to Jack and muttered, "Do you think it's right to play Tauronia games with other people? I mean . . . it's meant to be a secret, isn't it? Aunt Thea might be angry."

Jack snorted as the dinner lady dolloped some beans on his plate. "Yeah, right – like anyone here is ever going to believe that Tauronia is *real*!"

"Well, I know, but it seems a bit. . ." Lewis tailed off, not really sure what he meant to say. He loved their playground games and of course *nobody* would believe that Electrotaur and Slashermite and Grippakillataur and Stinkermite and all the other mad, dangerous, hilarious monsters they made up were real. Even though they were. Some months before, Jack and Lewis's drawings of Electrotaur and Slashermite had unexpectedly come to life in their bedroom, in the middle of the night, after getting splashed with magic mead. Since then, a whole host of other Taurs and Mites had sprung into being, in the underground world of Tauronia, which Jack and Lewis had also created.

"It's quite safe, you know," said Jack, collecting his cutlery and following Kevin off to the year five tables. "Go on – try telling someone. Tell them everything. They'll never believe you."

Lewis sat down with Henry. "You know Tauronia," he said, as they began to eat their fish fingers.

"Yeah – it's cool!" said Henry.

"It's actually real," said Lewis. "Me and Jack have been there. Electrotaur and Slashermite came to life after we spilled magic mead on the drawings we'd made of them. Remember that pylon that caught fire in the woods?" Henry nodded. "Electrotaur did that. He knocked out all the power to the town, too." Henry grinned and nodded.

"And then there was a guff-chasing monster that I made up," went on Lewis. "He chased our guffy cousin Timmy and put him in a bubble and. . ." Lewis trailed off. Henry was laughing and nodding and enjoying the story – but not for one second did he actually *believe* it. And why would he? Why would anyone? Their Aunt Thea was the only other person in the world who knew that the boys' monsters actually *had* come to life – she was the one who had given them the bottles of magic mead. Not that she had known the mead really *was* magic, back then.

Lewis would have *loved* to show Henry – and maybe William and Jacob and Ben, too. He'd love to get them all round Aunt Thea's house and introduce them to Slashermite, his very first come-to-life monster, who was purple with slashy claws and a rhino horn in the middle of his forehead, and Electrotaur whom Jack had drawn; a really scary-looking dragon-like character who glowed and sparked with electricity – but he knew he never could. Aunt Thea was right. It was just too dangerous.

"Let's see your pictures again," said Henry.

Lewis sighed and pulled the folder from his school bag, which he'd hung on the back of his chair. It was packed full of the drawings he and Jack had made of Tauronia and all the

Taurs and Mites that lived there. The drawings were slightly yellow in places, where the magic mead had been dripped on them, to bring the monsters to life.

"Cool!" said Henry, picking up a picture of Krushataur. "Bags I be Krushataur in the next game!"

"OK," said Lewis. "But Krushataur ends up falling down a chasm into molten custard. . ."

"Excuse *me*," said a prim voice across the other side of the dining hall, and Jack and Kevin groaned. It was Dahlia Dawkins and two of her friends – Kirsty Barker and Sarah Adams.

Jack and Kevin groaned. *Oh no! Dahlia! And her henchgirls!*

Dahlia sat down with her plate and her friends sat on either side of her, like ladies-in-waiting. Dahlia's school uniform was spotless and her hair was neatly cut so that it curled up at her collar like golden petals. Dahlia had big grey eyes and a little rosebud mouth and a shield-shaped badge on her blouse which read "MONITOR" and then a round badge which read "SCHOOL COUNCILLOR" and a square

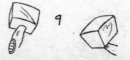

badge which read "PUPIL OF THE MONTH". She'd only been at the school for six weeks and she'd already become the most popular girl in year five.

Kirsty Barker, with brown plaits and a round face, gave a little tinkly giggle every time Dahlia said something and Sarah Adams, who was blonde and serious-looking, carried Dahlia's books for her but never said much.

"I wanted to have a word with you, Jack," said Dahlia, as she scooped peas on to her fork.

Jack stared at her, horror-struck. Dahlia Dawkins "having a word" with you was about as welcome as a rabid Rottweiler "having a bit of a play" with you.

"I am rather worried about the games you are playing," said Dahlia and Kirsty giggled nervously next to her.

Jack raised an eyebrow and speared a defenceless fish finger with more violence than was strictly necessary.

"I think they are rather a bad influence, especially on the year threes," continued Dahlia. "They're all about horrible, scary monsters and children getting eaten alive and heads exploding."

"Well, yeah – obviously," said Jack.

"Why do you always have to be so revolting?" asked Dahlia. "It doesn't always have to be about nasty creatures and bloodthirsty battles, does it? Why can't you do like *we* do and have some games which *don't* involve violence and . . . negativity?"

Jack and Kevin nearly choked on their breadcrumbs.

"I am starting up a campaign," said Dahlia. "It will be called the Play Nicely Campaign, or PNC for short. We will be campaigning to put a stop to nasty games."

Kirsty giggled and Sarah nodded gravely.

"So I hope you will make up nicer games in future," said Dahlia, with a sickly smile.

"You don't understand," said Jack. "We need horrible games! We need action! Riding around on pretend ponies all day might be huge excitement for you – but not us. Sooner or later we have to shoot at something. It's just the way we're made. And we only kill baddies, anyway."

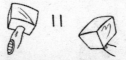

11

"Well, why can't you shoot bullets which turn baddies into goodies, then?" suggested Dahlia brightly. "That way you still get to shoot at something, but everyone ends up happy! You can all sit around together and have . . . cowboy's dinner . . . after the battle."

Jack looked at Kevin and they both sighed. Dahlia would never understand.

"OK," said Jack. "We'll turn them into goodies and have them for dinner."

Dahlia beamed and clapped her hands. "See! Is that so difficult?"

"No – but Henry will probably stick in my teeth a bit."

Dahlia squealed with frustration and stood up, gathering her plate and knife and fork.

"Just you wait," she warned, as Kirsty and Sarah stood up beside her. "I am taking this to the top! The teachers will support me! Miss Snippet has already said she will and so has Miss Budd. And some of the boys will too – they're not all like you and your brother! You *will* be stopped, or my name's not Dahlia Demelza Dawkins . . . just you wait!"

Chapter Two

Someone Special

Miss Budd smiled at the class. She smiled and smiled. She tilted her head to one side and smiled a bit more.

"Children! This is a very special week! It's special and it's lovely. I think it's going to be really lovely." Miss Budd cuddled her arms around her fluffy pink jumper in delight at all the loveliness that she was expecting.

"This is Someone Special Week. It's all about celebrating the people we care about – our friends, our families, our mum and dads ... even our teachers!" Miss Budd nodded and smiled a bit more. "Yes ... even teachers. Don't be shy! It was my idea, in fact, and Miss Stretch agreed that it was a lovely idea and I know you

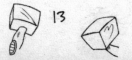

will think so too. Every day this week we will be celebrating 'Someone Special Week' in some way. Today we will make a collage of someone special in our lives, using scraps from the recycling bins. Tomorrow we will make love cakes to take to them. On Wednesday we will have a competition called Someone Special Idol Factor in which we can all vote for the *most* special, special someone in the school. On Thursday everyone will make friends with *everyone* – even people who are *not* friends at the moment because, you know what I always say – come on, everybody!"

Miss Budd raised her pink fluffy arms and proclaimed, "THAT'S NOT AN ENEMY! THAT'S JUST A FRIEND WE HAVEN'T MADE YET!" Nobody joined in.

"And best of all," went on Miss Budd, hugging Fluggles, her mascot fluffylump thing to her chest, "on Thursday you also get to bring someone special into the school! Someone from your family, like Mummy or Daddy or Granny or Aunty. . ."

Aunty? Lewis's eyes lit up. He grinned. Just wait till he told Jack!

"And perhaps some of them can tell the class all about their interesting lives! Won't that be lovely?"

The class smiled back and one of Lewis's Friends He Hadn't Made Yet threw a metal ruler at the back of his head. Lewis decided to make a collage of him. Out of chewed-up toilet roll and earwax.

At the end of the day Lewis caught up with Jack as he crossed the playground. "Hey! Guess what? We can bring Aunt Thea into school with us on Thursday!"

Jack turned around. "Aunt Thea? Here? Why?"

"It's Someone Special Week – didn't you know?"

"Aah yes – *that*!" replied Jack, wincing. "We've got to write caring poems. And plant a flower. And send up a balloon with a loving message to the world on it. Dahlia Dawkins is organizing it all." He shuddered. "Oh no – there she is now! Better watch out, Lewis – she's after you too!"

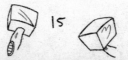

Dahlia Dawkins was standing at the school gate with several other girls, including Kirsty and Sarah. They were all waving little bits of paper. Dahlia spotted them and stalked over, looking grand and triumphant. "Here you are!" she said and handed each of them a bit of paper. On the paper they read:

16

**HELP US TAKE THE VIOLENCE
OUT OF PLAYTIME**

Underneath, alongside a column of little blobs, Jack read:

HELP US TO STOP CERTAIN PUPILS FROM:

- pretending to shoot each other
- pretending to decapitate each other
- pretending to pull each other's entrails out with a rusty fork in the dining hall
- talking about wars, battles, snipers, mad axe murderers and killer monsters

LET'S ALL PLAY NICELY!

There followed a row of arrows to indicate that the paper should be flipped over. Jack flipped it and on the other side he read:

SUGGESTED GAMES FOR PLAYING NICELY, AS AGREED BY MISS STRETCH:

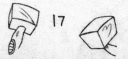

17

- Mountain rescuers (who always rescue people in time)
- Doctors (who always save lives in time)
- Good knights (who are kind to dragons and princesses)
- Horse-riders (who never kick their horses with spurs on)
- Finger-knitting
- Yu-Be-Nice card collecting and swapping (no duelling)

"Finger-knitting?" spluttered Lewis. "What on earth is *finger*-knitting?"

Dahlia waved her hand. Kirsty leaped forward with a basket of wool. "Choose any colour you like," she giggled. "Tomorrow I will be giving finger-knitting lessons in the playground at break. It's fun."

Lewis stared, aghast, at the basket full of wool. The balls of yarn were all in girl colours. "And I would want to do this . . . because. . .?"

"Because," cut in Dahlia, turning him around and stuffing some of the wool into his

18

school backpack, despite his struggles, "you'll be needing something else to do – other than your usual negative, violent, horrible games. Miss Stretch says so too. I told you!"

Jack dropped the bits of paper in a puddle and stood on them. "Never," he said. "You will never stop us doing what we do. We've got just as much right to play our games as you have. You stay out of ours and we'll stay out of yours!"

Dahlia turned quickly away, into a huddle with her girls. "I haven't got time to argue with you today, Jack," she called back. "We're moving house. And anyway, arguing is negative and I am always positive – that's why I'm Pupil of the Month. You'll soon see that we're right. Come on, girls!" She led them all away, cantering and whinnying, Kirsty carrying her basket of wool on the back of her imaginary pony and all of them pulling gently on imaginary reins.

"That pony thing is really weird!" muttered Lewis. "I've got a bad feeling about this. They'll be wanting us to brush each other's hair next."

Jack shivered. He too had the feeling that

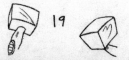

19

something unpleasant was coming . . . and he didn't think it was finger-knitting.

"And what on earth are Yu-Be-Nice cards?" snorted Lewis.

Jack dug into his pocket and pulled a card out to show his brother. It was an ordinary duelling game card, which had been doctored by Dahlia and her henchgirls. It looked familiar . . . Lewis had this card in one of his duelling card collections. Normally it had a dragon-like creature holding a sword. It had once read:

CRIMSON BLADE

- 2000 destruction points
- Fast on its feet, a Crimson Blade can rip you to shreds with blade or claws
- Weaknesses:
1. A Crimson Blade cannot see a foe unless it moves
2. Its sense of smell is limited

There was a sticker over the old information. Now it read:

CRIMSON BLISS

- 2000 popularity points
- Fast on its feet, a Crimson Bliss can dance like a prima ballerina and is always dressed in lovely red frocks and matching shoes
- Weaknesses: It cannot help cuddling kittens and this sometimes leads to claw marks on its frocks

The dragon had been drawn over, so that its sword was now a cascade of flowers and its fearsome grimace was a kindly smile. It had long curly Biro eyelashes. Lewis stared up at his brother, horrified. "This is so *wrong*."

Jack nodded. "They've been handing them out all afternoon. But what's worse is that the teachers are encouraging them."

Lewis shook his head. "It's mind control! That's what it is. We must *fight* to stop it!"

"Yeah," muttered Jack darkly, "as long as it's only with love bombs, cuddle swords and goodie bullets. . ."

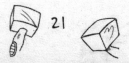

Chapter Three

Puppies and Petals

"You know, they do have a point," said Aunt Thea. Jack and Lewis gaped at her, appalled.

"Well, you don't have to look at me like I've just hit you with The Brick Of Horror," she huffed, twisting her long red hair into a high ponytail in front of the hallway mirror. "I agree that defacing dragons and making them cuddle kittens is rather ghastly, but the fact is, you *are* both terribly bloodthirsty! And think of what happens! Only a few weeks ago poor Electrotaur got his arm nearly bitten off by Grippakillataur, to say nothing of how close your cousin came to being a Krushataur kebab."

Jack and Lewis looked sulky. How could Aunt Thea side with the revolting Dahlia

22

Dawkins and her henchgirls?

"I'm *not* siding with Daisy or whatever her name is," said Aunt Thea, as if she'd read their minds. "I'm sure she and her friends are quite dreadful – but the fact is you two *are* always making up horribly gruesome creatures and that's what makes Tauronia so dangerous. If you'd made up some Taurs which were a bit nicer, then maybe I wouldn't have had to ban you from going down into Tauronia . . . but it's too late now. It's unspeakably dangerous thanks to your lurid imaginations."

Jack and Lewis folded their arms and looked even sulkier, but they had to admit that Aunt Thea was right. The one time they'd been into Tauronia – only because it was a terrible emergency – they had all nearly died a horrible death. They could easily have been drowned in hot custard or pulped in the massive jaws of Grippakillataur or had their heads popped like grapes in the huge pincers of Krushataur.

"Oh do cheer up," laughed Aunt Thea, turning away from the mirror and mussing their hair. "Come and do some more drawings while

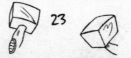

I make hot chocolate. Then you can draw open the door in the standing stone and Electrotaur and Slashermite can come up to play."

Jack and Lewis set to work at the kitchen table while the wonderful aroma of cocoa and warm milk filled the air. Lewis went to take the folder of all their drawings out of his school bag, so they could add their new ones when they were finished and meaded.

"Oh poo!" he said. "I left the Tauronia folder at school. I thought I'd put it in my bag."

"You shouldn't take that to school!" scolded Jack. "You might lose it! And then we might forget some of the stuff that's in Tauronia!"

"I just wanted to show Henry," protested Lewis. "It'll be in my desk, still, I'm sure."

"Jack's right," said Aunt Thea. "You should leave it here with me – keep it safe. Those drawings are very precious."

Jack gave Lewis a hard stare. "Sorry," said Lewis. "I'll bring it back tomorrow and I won't take it in again."

"I've got new neighbours, by the way," said Aunt Thea. "So we will have to be extra careful about where we play with Electrotaur and Slashermite. There is one part of the garden where they *could* be seen from the bathroom window next door, so we must make sure they walk very close to the hedge to get past it unseen."

"Who's moving in?" asked Jack as he began to draw.

"Don't know yet," replied Aunt Thea, stirring the hot chocolate in a saucepan. "A removals van showed up this morning and I think everything's been taken in. But I haven't seen the new people yet. I'll pop round with some apple crumble later, to say hello. Here you go."

She put two blue mugs filled with hot chocolate on the table, sending fragrant curls of steam across Jack's spectacles. He took them off to wipe them and then replaced them so he could get back to Wuffamite.

Wuffamite was basically a shaggy brown puppy that stood up on two legs like a human. Most of the time he was cheerful and liked to play fetch. Jack suddenly felt embarrassed. In spite of everything he felt about Dahlia and her plans to make them "play nicely" he had just

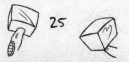

created a monster which was much fluffier than usual. Was her mind control working on him? He decided to make Wuffamite's tail super-deadly just to spite Dahlia. If you pulled it he turned into Wolfataur – a huge, ferocious, rabid wolf-creature. Its teeth were needle-sharp and its breath smelled like a hundred tins of cheap dog food opened up and left in the sun.

Wuffamite/Wolfataur's quest, thought Jack (for all Taurs and Mites needed a quest), would be to remind people that even soppy, fluffy, ever-so-nice things have their nasty side and shouldn't be messed with. Even kittens had claws and liked to drag mice around by their tails. Probably Dahlia hadn't noticed that.

Aunt Thea cradled her mug of cocoa and peered at Lewis's drawing. "That's lovely, Lewis. What's it called?"

"It's Flowertaur," said Lewis, looking up at his aunt with a sweet smile. On his paper was a tall, gangly creature with big round violet eyes and a beaming red mouth. Its head looked like a sunflower, with yellow petals all around it and its arms and legs were sprouting lots of green leaves and the occasional yellow bud. "He likes to go around Tauronia planting little flowers along the river banks," went on Lewis.

"Well, he's absolutely wonderful," said Aunt Thea. "Which just goes to show that you *can* make up nice things. What's yours, Jack?"

Jack told her about Wuffamite. He didn't mention the killer tail or the bad breath. Aunt Thea beamed at him too. "I'll get the mead," she said.

Jack and Lewis looked at each other.

"*Flower*taur?" mouthed Jack in disgust.

"*Wuffa*mite?" Lewis mouthed back, reading the name on Jack's drawing.

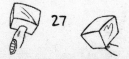

Aunt Thea returned and poured a few drops of Merrion's Mead on to their drawings.

Jack grinned as the magic yellow liquid dribbled across his drawing, sending up a lovely sweet smell of fermented honey. He liked to imagine Wuffamite springing to life down in Tauronia and wondered how he would get on. Slashermite was always good at reporting back on how any new Taurs were doing.

"OK," said Aunt Thea, when it was done. "They'll be appearing in Tauronia any time now. You can draw open the door in the standing stone now – and I'll go and collect Electrotaur and Slashermite and guide them past the dodgy bit of the garden."

She went off at once while Jack swiftly drew an open door in a big chunk of serpentine rock – the same as the one that stood tall at the end of Aunt Thea's garden, like a giant crooked finger beckoning to the sky. This was the main portal to Tauronia and a door appeared in it only after they had drawn it open and "meaded" it. As Jack carefully poured a couple of drops of mead on to the drawing, Lewis screwed his eyes up at him.

 28

"Wuffamite?" he said again. "That's a bit lame, isn't it? Trying to get into Dahlia's good books now, are we?"

"You're a fine one to talk," retorted Jack. "*Flower*taur? Dahlia would *love* that!"

"Well, I didn't mention the poison-tipped flying thorns to Aunt Thea, obviously," said Lewis. "Flowertaur *is* very pretty. But he's also an assassin."

"Oh," said Jack. "Fair enough. And Wuffamite, just so you know, has a killer tail which turns him into Wolfataur – a rabid wolf-monster – if you pull it. He's got teeth like needles and breath that'll make you heave if he opens his mouth even six feet away from you."

"I SICKEN," said a stern voice and they looked up to see Electrotaur ducking through the kitchen door. Although he stood as tall and proud as ever, flexing his lightning-shaped fingers and sending little sparks of electricity out of his green eyes, he did look a bit pale around the golden scales of his dragon-like mouth.

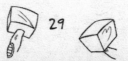

29

Slashermite scampered in after him, his finger-blades wafting about in the air rather agitatedly. Purple, shiny and only as tall as Lewis, he was full of energy. He was not really a frightening creature – even though he did have a fearsome rhino horn on his forehead and viciously sharp blades on his hands that could shred a sofa to ribbons in seconds. But right now Slashermite also looked a bit off colour. His tail, with its green curl, was rather limp.

"We just met Wuffamite on the way up to Overworld," gulped Slashermite. "I wanted to play. I pulled his tail. He turned into a ravenous wolf-beast, tried to eat me and then made us both feel sick with his breath. Ugh!"

"Oops," said Jack. "Sorry – forgot to draw your immunity in. Here," he scribbled some words on his latest picture and dribbled a little more mead on to them. "You're sorted."

Jack and Lewis cared very much about their first ever Taurs and realized they needed to take better care of them after Electrotaur had lost an arm in Grippakillataur's mouth. Jack had later redrawn and re-meaded poor Electrotaur's arm, but the whole thing had been traumatic. Now Jack and Lewis always made sure that Electrotaur and Slashermite had protection from whatever their creators had just dreamed up and meaded.

Immediately, Electrotaur became his usual colour around the mouth. He was a splendid creature, at eight foot tall. If he got angry he was like a walking firework display and could electrocute you with one touch of his lightning claws. This made him a little dangerous and so, not long after creating him, Jack had amended his drawing of Electrotaur to include a dial in his Taur's chest with which to turn down his power or, if necessary, to cut it out altogether – like putting a TV on standby.

The only design fault now left on Electrotaur was his trousers. They had been intended to look like a scary criss-cross of wild electrical fire whipping around his legs . . . but just before the mead first got spilled on Jack's picture, he had been thinking that these fiery legs actually looked more like a pair of his granddad's golfing trousers. Or even those worn by Rupert Bear. So the mighty Electrotaur ended up in rather dodgy checked slacks. It was the *dream* that came to life, rather than the actual drawing, it seemed – although it always needed to start with a drawing. Jack kept meaning to redraw those trousers, but something always got in the way.

"Hot chocolate, you two?" asked Aunt Thea, even though she knew Electrotaur would decline. He only ever drank electricity. Aunt Thea kept packs of batteries in the drawer in case he got thirsty, although he usually took a drink from his lightning fountain, down in Tauronia, before coming up to see them.

"Yes please, Lady Thea!" said Slashermite. Slashermite had no clothing problems. His shiny purple skin was all he wore. He was a well-behaved Mite who mostly kept his razor-sharp finger-blades tucked in and well clear of Aunt Thea's furniture and carpets, despite his overwhelming urge to slash. He got on extremely well with Lewis. Electrotaur was a lot less playful, but a formidable warrior who had rescued them from danger more than once. Jack was proud of him, even if he couldn't roll around the lawn playing rough games with him.

"Do you feel better now, Leccy?" he asked and his creation nodded stiffly. Jack picked up his crayon. It really was time to sort out that trouser problem. Then he remembered that the drawing of Electrotaur was in the

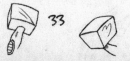

folder which Lewis had left at school.

He was just about to start telling Lewis off again about that when the doorbell went. Everyone froze.

"Right," said Aunt Thea, heading for the hallway. "Everybody sit still and be absolutely silent!"

They all sat down, staring at each other nervously, except Electrotaur, who towered, motionless, by the kitchen sink, his electrical energy making the draining board vibrate slightly.

They heard Aunt Thea open the front door. "Oh – *hello*! You must be my new neighbours."

"Yes, we are," replied a crisp, posh voice. "We thought it would be polite to come and introduce ourselves. My name is Doris – and this is my daughter."

"Well, how nice to meet you both. I'm Aramathea Casterbridge. I was going to pop around and say hello myself." There was a slightly awkward pause, during which Aunt Thea would normally have said, "Do come in!" Today, however, with a small purple slashing thing with a rhino horn and a huge golden, blue-sparking dragon-like thing both camped in her kitchen, this was a little difficult.

"Oh – you must think me rude!" laughed Aunt Thea after a few seconds. "I would love to invite you in for a cup of tea but . . . well . . . the kitchen has just flooded! My – my washing machine has sprung a leak . . . Would you like to come back in a couple of hours and have tea and apple crumble? I was just about to make one for you."

"Oh, we couldn't put you to such trouble," said Doris graciously. "We just wanted to say hello."

"But we can help you mop up if you like," came a trilling younger voice which made the hairs stand up on the back of Jack's neck. "You mustn't let your kitchen floor get ruined. Here – I can make a start!"

Then there was a fearful gasp and a squeak from Aunt Thea and a scuffle and fast footsteps ringing across the wooden floor of the hallway. Three seconds later, despite Aunt Thea's cry of

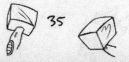

"No – please – come back!" something quite astonishing and dreadful happened.

Into the kitchen stepped Dahlia Dawkins.

Chapter Four

Madeupgamenotrealatall

Dahlia's round grey eyes grew to the size of dinner plates – or so it seemed. Her mouth grew into a similar shape as she took in the monsters in Aunt Thea's kitchen, and Jack and Lewis sitting staring back at her with identical faces of horror.

"Really . . ." called Aunt Thea in a wobbly voice, "I'd rather you didn't. It's not safe. The machine's still switched on. . . You might get . . . electrocuted."

"Dahlia!" called her mother. "Come back at once. It's not polite to barge into someone's house even if we have come out of good manners. Miss Casterbridge obviously has better things to do."

Dahlia opened her mouth but nothing came out except a very quiet "Wee . . . eh . . . uuh . . .

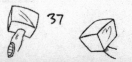

37

eh. . ." which only the occupants of the kitchen could hear, in their shocked, frozen silence.

Lewis suddenly scrambled to his feet and grabbed Dahlia's wrist. He yanked her in front of Slashermite and as she dragged in a deep breath and got ready to scream her pretty little lungs inside out, he whispered, "Slashy! Quick! Hypnotize her to think this is just a made-up game – and not real at all!"

Slashermite wafted his finger-blades back and forth at high speed in front of Dahlia's stunned face. "Thisisjustamadeupgameandnotrealatall,"

he hissed. Dahlia blinked and then looked at Jack and Lewis with pursed lips. "Oh!" she said. "*You* two. I might have known!"

Jack grabbed her arm and steered her back into the hallway where Aunt Thea was standing by the door, trying to stop Doris Dawkins from following her daughter into the house.

"Look, Mummy," said Dahlia. "It's one of those boys I was telling you about. The ones who are always making up nasty violent games at school!"

"Oh," said Doris Dawkins, managing to smile and look disapproving at the same time. "Well, I'm sure they'll be playing nice games from now on, now that you've sorted playtime activities out, Dahlia."

"Oh yes," grinned Jack. "We will. Tomorrow we will only play Flowertaur and Wuffamite! They're ever so lovely! Thanks for the Yu-Be-Nice card, Dahlia."

"You're welcome," said Dahlia, nodding primly. "Well . . . I suppose we're neighbours now."

"No – we just come here to visit our aunt sometimes," said Jack, shoving her out of the door. "You'll probably never bump into us again."

"Well – very nice to meet you," said Doris,

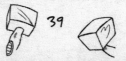

frostily. "I'm sure we won't need to trouble you in future."

"No, really – no trouble," gasped Aunt Thea. "And do come back later for tea and crumble."

"I'm sure we couldn't possibly. You have enough to sort out with your kitchen . . . and your nephews." And, nodding snootily at them, Doris turned and walked down the path with Dahlia.

"Bye then . . ." said Aunt Thea, before closing the door and collapsing against it, weak with shock. She raised her brown eyes to Jack, and Lewis, who had now come into the hallway. "What on earth did you do? I thought the game was well and truly up!"

Lewis grinned. "High speed hypnotism from Slashy! He was brilliant. I've never seen him do it so fast." Lewis had given Slashermite the power of hypnosis, but he could only use it when Lewis asked him to.

"And you're quite sure it worked?" Aunt Thea walked back into the kitchen, looking terribly worried.

"Well she didn't scream, did she? And she was perfectly OK coming out again, wasn't she?" said Jack.

"Yes . . . yes it does look as if we got away with it. Next time, boys, will you remind me to just ignore the doorbell. It's not worth the risk. Imagine if she had started screaming and then run away before we could get Slashermite to work on her! Imagine! And her mother would have been in like a shot and then . . . oh! You know, sometimes I think I am such a bad aunt. I should really have flushed all that mead down the toilet long ago. It's only because I trust you both never to use it in the real world that I haven't done exactly that. Do you know what could happen if you ever did? Do you know what awful danger could result? It just doesn't bear thinking about."

"It doesn't bear thinking about that Dahlia's living next door," grunted Jack.

"Well, she won't be back, by the looks of it. I've not made a good impression on her mother at all." Aunt Thea sighed. "I so rarely *do* make a good impression on mothers."

"Well, you can make a good impression on lots of people this week," said Lewis, suddenly remembering.

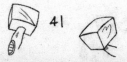

"How so?" asked Aunt Thea.

"By coming to school with me on Thursday. It's Someone Special Week, and we're allowed to bring someone special into school with us. So can you come? Can you?"

Aunt Thea blinked. "Well, Lewis, that's very touching. I'd love to . . . but don't you think you ought to ask your mum? Or dad?"

"Can't," said Jack. "Dad'll be at the office and Mum works at the tourist information bureau in the mornings. You haven't got a deadline or anything, have you?"

"No," Aunt Thea smiled. She was a travel writer and typed out long stories about the places she visited for newspapers and magazines. "I just finished my piece on Cadiz – so I'm fine for a few days."

"Oh good – so you can come!" said Lewis. "And please bring stuff . . . you know . . . weird stuff from your travels."

Aunt Thea nodded slowly. "Well . . . the legal stuff, at any rate."

On the way back home for tea, Jack and Lewis

worried about their school playtime games of the future.

"Do you think everyone will really start behaving like Dahlia and her girls?" muttered Lewis.

"No – never," said Jack, but he didn't sound very certain. "Not our gang." He stopped and stared at his brother. "I know! We'll just make up a code!"

"A code?"

"Yes – we'll make up our own language and code and stuff . . . so that when we say something, the Play Nicely lot will think it means something else. Like . . . instead of 'I'm going to bash the top of your head off with my sabre' . . . which is, well, you know . . . kind of obvious . . . we can say, 'I'm going to brush your hair with my best brush . . . and remove your scrunchie!'"

"But that actually *means* bash the top of your head off!" shouted Lewis, joyfully. "And they'll never know!"

"Exactly!"

"And instead of 'I'm going to run you right through with my sword until you expire, you evil dog'," went on Jack, warming to his theme,

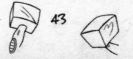

"it'll be 'I'm going to tickle your ribs until you scream with laughter, you naughty puppy'."

Lewis gurgled with mirth. "And instead of 'Die, fool!' we can say 'Take a nap now, Snuffles!'"

"OK – we have to write these all down, ready to hand out to our gang tomorrow," said Jack. "This is going to be brilliant!"

The next day at school, while Lewis was making love cakes for someone special, he smuggled little bits of paper to Henry and William and Ben, listing all the coded phrases they needed to carry on playing their usual Tauronia games without making the Play Nicely Campaigners suspicious. Henry read his while Miss Budd was showing them how to dollop cake mixture into the little flowery cake cases.

"Who's laughing?" demanded Miss Budd, pausing with the mixture dripping slowly off her spoon.

"It was me, miss," said Lewis quickly, kicking Henry on the leg. They mustn't get found out before they'd even tried the code!

"And can we all share the joke, Lewis?" Miss Budd stared at him reprovingly.

"Oh – it's . . . it's not a joke . . . it's just that my love cake goo was making slurpy noises," fibbed Lewis.

"Mixture, Lewis," corrected Miss Budd. "Not goo."

Dahlia was staring at him. She definitely was. Jack shuddered and tried to concentrate on his caring poem. So far, all he'd got down was:

> You are someone special
> Because you're very kind to me
> This poem's to say thank you . . .

And all he could think of to finish it was "And now I need a wee" – which would probably not get him a very good mark. But every time he glanced up towards Dahlia

and her henchgirls, Dahlia was either staring at him or glancing away from *having* been staring at him. It made him terribly uneasy. He knew she couldn't possibly think that what she'd witnessed in Aunt Thea's kitchen was real . . . but even so.

"OK, everyone," called out Miss White. "I think you've all had enough time to complete your caring poems now. I think it's time we read some out." There was a chorus of groans from the boys, followed by a wave of excited squeaks from the girls. "Dahlia," said Miss White, "perhaps you'd like to start us off."

Dahlia smiled sweetly and got to her feet. She held out her poem, written in curly purple letters. Jack could see that all the dots on the "i"s were little hearts.

"To Someone Special," sighed Dahlia and Kirsty giggled with excited joy while Sarah just stared up at her in wonder.

"There is someone special in my life
Someone who doesn't know
Who thinks up amazing stories

And makes wonderful creatures grow
The stories are made of caring
And the wonderful creatures, of love
A bottle of happiness brings them to life
Like the light of the sun from above."

Dahlia held her free hand aloft like a ballet dancer and smirked. Kirsty giggled. Sarah stared. The class clapped.

Jack fell off his chair and hit his head so hard on the desk next him that he had to be taken to the school nurse.

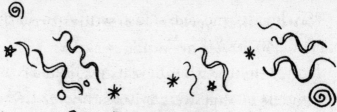

Chapter Five

Killing Nicely

"She knows!" Jack grabbed Lewis the minute he came out of the lower-school door and hauled him off behind the bins. "She knows! SHE KNOWS!"

Lewis stared at Jack. His brother had a big red bump on the right side of his forehead and his eyes looked glassy and filled with panic.

"What are you on about? What happened to your head?"

"She knows!" repeated Jack. "Dahlia – she *knows* about the Taurs! She just as good as told the whole class!"

"But she can't," said Lewis. "Slashy hypnotized her. You saw it!"

48

"So how come she's just written a caring poem all about it?"

Jack explained what he'd heard to Lewis and Lewis gulped and began to look pretty panicked himself.

"Are you *sure*?" he whispered. "I mean – you've just had a nasty bump to the head. Maybe you dreamed about this 'bottle of happiness' thing."

"I nearly knocked myself out *because* of the 'bottle of happiness' thing!" retorted Jack. "I'm not a total noobstick!"

"So . . . she *saw* Electrotaur and Slashermite and we didn't get her properly hypnotized to forget . . . because there wasn't time," mused Lewis. "But how would she know about the bottle of magic mead? Even if she saw it, she wouldn't know what it was . . . would she? How could she know about Tauronia?"

"Maybe she's just been spying on us and overheard our games and put two and two together and . . .' Jack shook his head. "None of this makes sense! If she knew it was *real*, where was all the screaming and phoning the police and stuff?"

"Maybe Slashy just hypnotized her enough to stop her panicking," suggested Lewis. "So she hasn't *needed* to start screaming or calling the police."

"Yes, that could be it," gulped Jack.

"Well . . . that's not so bad, then."

"Not so *bad*? Dahlia Dawkins – knowing about our Taurs?"

"So – what can she do about it?" said Lewis. "She can't prove it. Let's just ignore her and go and play. We'll have to work out a way to get her in front of Slashy again soon, so we can sort it out – but for now we've got to act normal."

Henry and Kevin were waiting, with much excitement, to get on with playing Tauronia, using the codes that Jack and Lewis had come up with.

"I'm going to brush your hair with my best brush," threatened Henry, with vicious slashing movements and an evil grin. "And remove your scrunchie!"

Jack and Lewis laughed and did their best to join in, but a short distance away, Dahlia and her henchgirls sat, making very long wiggly woolly things out of girly-coloured yarn. They had even got some of the boys involved. Ben was holding up a small yellow worm dangling from his forefinger in the breeze. He was whimpering. The end of his finger was turning blue, because his finger-knitting was too violent and he'd pulled the wool dangerously tight.

"There'll be gangrene before the day is out," muttered Jack darkly, as he fended off Kevin's attempts to kill him in a very nice way.

After five minutes all the boys gave up and slumped down at the foot of the Indian bean tree.

"It's no good," said Kevin. "It's just not fun any more. I might as well go and join the finger-knitters. Maybe we could make a spitting cobra!" he added brightly. Henry followed him.

All around the playground, boys were losing hope. With dinner ladies and girl spies listening in on their games and reporting any of them for playing nastily, enjoying themselves the way they always had was becoming impossible. Some boys were just playing football, but even they were being told that everyone should have a chance to score a goal – and the goalkeeper was made to move to one side and keep his hands in his pockets every so often, to give everyone a fair chance and not be negative.

"How's it going, then?" Jack and Lewis looked up to see henchgirl Sarah Adams standing a little way off, twisting a tortured-looking bit of purple wool in her fingers.

"How do you *think*?" grunted Jack.

Sarah looked at her feet. "You know, it's not that we don't like . . . adventure games. We do! I mean, I do. It's just all the . . . you know . . . killing."

"Whatever," said Jack.

"I mean, if there was a bit less of that entrails stuff going on . . . maybe we could all play together," added Sarah with a watery smile.

"Yeah, right. *Girls* playing Tauronia," sneered Lewis.

Sarah shrugged and glanced over her shoulder. "I just came over, really, to ask if you've seen my little bead purse," she said, looking back at Lewis and Jack. They shrugged back at her. She sighed. "Just thought I'd ask. It's pink and blue . . . just in case you see it. It's a bit special." She turned and walked back to Dahlia.

Dahlia smiled at Jack and Lewis and gave them a wave. Her smile seemed very *knowing*.

"She must have sent Sarah over to spy on us," muttered Jack. "Lost bead purse, my foot!"

"I don't believe it for one moment," said Aunt Thea after school that day.

"You weren't *there*!" protested Jack. He was too agitated even to drink his hot chocolate.

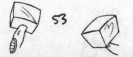

"I think that maybe something is going on with her – *subconsciously* – but she can't possibly believe that monsters are real," said Aunt Thea. "Nobody believes it."

Jack and Lewis looked at each other and then sat down at the kitchen table, brooding.

"Oh, do stop looking so worried! I saw Dahlia on her way to school this morning. She gave me a friendly wave and even her stuck-up mother gave me a nod. I can't believe we'd be on waving and nodding terms if they thought I was harbouring an eight-foot buzzing electricity beast and a small but terrifying, slashing monster."

Jack had to admit she was probably right. "It's just the thing about the bottle, in her poem . . . that's what made me really freak," he said.

"She was just being poetic. Lots of people talk about bottles and such like in poems . . ." said Aunt Thea. "And even if she *did* believe in Electrotaur and Slashermite, how would she know about the mead bottles?"

"We had one out on the table," said Jack.

"She still couldn't know what was in it – or that it was magic! And I find it hard to believe that with your two Taurs staring at her she could possibly have noticed anything else. Just relax, both of you. The only people who know that the mead in those bottles brings your drawings to life are you and me. And speaking of drawings, have you brought your folder back from school yet, Lewis? Your new drawings need to go into it, and then it needs to go safely back in the drawer."

Lewis bit his lip. "Umm – no. I looked in my tray at school but it wasn't there. It must be at home somewhere. Maybe Mum took it out when she pulled out my PE kit for washing yesterday, before we came over to see you."

There came a banging noise and a high-pitched drone through the polished wood plank walls of Aunt Thea's kitchen.

Aunt Thea sighed. "They're not losing any time getting on with the DIY at any rate. They were both banging around upstairs till all hours last night and here they go again. I swear they were even floorboarding their attic during the ten o'clock news! Very energetic for just the two of them. No sign of a Mr Dawkins at all. I think he may be in the Navy or some such. I hear they've moved around quite a lot."

"Well hopefully they'll move around again, soon," said Jack. "We'd better get home for tea. Don't forget you're coming into school on Thursday, Aunty."

"Of course not," said Aunt Thea. "I'm looking forward to it."

After her nephews had left, Aunt Thea resolved that Jack and Lewis must leave Electrotaur and Slashermite down in Tauronia for a few days, until everything had settled down and they all felt a bit less nervous.

Chapter Six

Sweet Pink Horror

That night Jack dreamed of Dahlia Dawkins. She was holding his hand, playing ring-a-ring o' roses with him and Lewis, Electrotaur and Slashermite. She was smiling like a little angel and singing sweetly while her golden petals of hair floated in the breeze. As they all went round and round Jack noticed that Slashermite's finger-blades had turned into marshmallows and there was a rose growing out of his head, where his rhino horn had been. Then he saw that Electrotaur had orange sequins all over his scales.

He shot up in bed and shouted "NO!" at exactly the same time as Lewis.

Their "NO!"s rang around their bedroom and for a few seconds they both sat there,

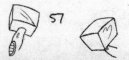

breathing raggedly, waiting for Mum or Dad to crash in, wondering what the emergency was. Their parents were deep sleepers, though, and neither of them seemed to have woken up.

"I just had a terrible dream," gulped Lewis. "Dahlia Dawkins was in it!"

"Me too – with you and me and Electrotaur . . ."

"And Slashermite!" joined in Lewis.

Jack hung over the edge of his top bunk and stared down at his brother. "Ring-a-ring o' roses?" he breathed. Lewis nodded. "Slashy's horn was a rose!" he whimpered.

"It's OK. It was just a dream," said Jack, but he felt as OK as a big wobbly plate of blancmange. "Although it's weird to both have the same one . . . what's that about?"

"Marshmallows for finger-blades!" muttered Lewis.

"Sequins on Electrotaur!" hissed back Jack, shaking his head. "Something's wrong. Something's badly wrong! Come on. We've got to get over to Aunt Thea's."

By the pale green light of their digital clock,

 58

which read 1.55 a.m., Jack and Lewis pulled jumpers on over their pyjamas, and socks and trainers on to their feet. It wasn't a cold night, so they didn't worry about coats, but each grabbed a torch from their sock drawer.

It wasn't the first time they'd gone through the woods to Aunt Thea's by moonlight. It was the most direct way to go even if it was very dark and full of trip-ups. If they went by the roads they might get spotted – and no grown-up would let a seven-year-old and a nine-year-old go walking off in the night without stopping them.

There was very little moonlight, but their torches guided them along the familiar path

to Aunt Thea's, past The Holes and the little muddy stream with the abandoned pram and across to the far side of the wood where the river separated them from the row of cottages Aunt Thea lived in. They were in luck – it had been a dry month, so the stepping stones were high and clear of the shallow river, and they ran across without getting wet.

At Aunt Thea's door, Jack paused. He knew the doorbell battery was gone. Last week, when Electrotaur had been extra thirsty for electricity, they'd run out of batteries and Aunt Thea had sighed and popped the double A one out of the doorbell, to keep Electrotaur quiet. He could have gone up the garden, nipped back into the standing stone and got himself a lightning fountain drink back down in Tauronia, but it was raining and windy and nobody wanted to open the kitchen door. So Jack couldn't ring the bell . . . and knocking when Dahlia Dawkins could be asleep next door – only metres away – was dangerous.

Jack stepped back and peered up at Aunt Thea's bedroom window. "We'll have to chuck stones," he whispered to Lewis. "Just little ones!" They both picked up handfuls of gravel from Aunt Thea's rockery and hurled them high up at her window. The gravel rattled against the glass, sounding terrifyingly loud, and they held their breath. Nothing. After a few seconds they threw more gravel. This time a light went on and then their aunt's sleepy face appeared between the curtains and she stared down at them in disbelief.

A minute later the front door opened. Jack and Lewis shuffled inside. Aunt Thea was standing in the hallway, wearing her green silk dressing gown, her red hair all wild around her head and shoulders. She narrowed her eyes at them. "This had better be good!"

"Something's terribly wrong," said Jack. "We need to see Electrotaur and Slashermite – now!"

"Jack! It's half past two in the morning!" spluttered Aunt Thea. "Could it not possibly wait until daytime?"

"No! It can't. We've had a dream about something awful happening to them." Jack

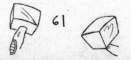

shoved his aunt along to the kitchen. "They've gone all girly and sweet and it's all to do with Dahlia Dawkins."

"Jack! Having a *bad dream* is no good reason to go running across the woods in the dead of night and wake up a relative! You do have a mum and dad for that, you know!"

"We have to get Electrotaur and Slashermite up – right away! Please, Aunty. Lewis and I have been dreaming about them – and it's not good!"

Aunt Thea closed her eyes with a sigh. "I had made my mind up that we were going to steer clear of Merrion's Mead and all this Tauronia stuff for quite a while. It just doesn't feel safe right now, with the new neighbours."

"Oh, *please*, just this once!" Lewis begged, doing his biggest eyes and most appealingly pathetic smile.

"Well, as it's dark and there's not much chance of them being seen, I suppose so. But only very quickly, so you two can set your minds at rest over this silly dream business. Come on – get to it!" Aunt Thea opened her tall cupboard and brought down one of the five twiggy wooden bottles of Merrion's Mead which stood in a row at the back of the cupboard. Jack worried every time he saw them. There used to be six. One day another bottle would be empty. And then another. And then, one day, it would all run out. Aunt Thea didn't know if there was any more in the world. She had tried to find out, but nobody seemed to know about it, and the old Welsh shopkeeper who had sold them to her had retired and left the country.

Lewis was already drawing the portal to Tauronia. Jack unlatched the kitchen door.

"Absolute silence bringing them back through the garden," warned Aunt Thea. "And keep close to the hedge."

The standing stone portal was open by the time Jack reached it, sending a golden shaft of light up into the garden. The metallic scratches on stone Jack could hear were Slashermite's sharply bladed feet, and the steady thudding step came from Electrotaur's chunky clawed toes, as the odd couple of friends made their way up the spiral stone

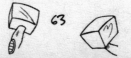

staircase from their world to Jack's.

"Shhh!" said Jack, as soon as they emerged. "Don't make any noise. We've got to get to the house without being seen or heard."

The Taurs didn't argue with him. Jack reckoned, even in the dim light, that he could see anxious looks on both their faces. They all went back down the garden, Electrotaur ducking under Aunt Thea's willow arch and Slashermite swiping a few overgrown twigs off her privet hedge in passing (he liked to help keep the garden neat) and a minute later they were back in the kitchen, where Aunt Thea and Lewis waited edgily.

"OK – sit down, everyone," said Aunt Thea. "This shouldn't take long. Electrotaur, Slashermite," she continued as they all drew a chair up to the kitchen table. "Jack and Lewis have some notion that you're in trouble, because they had a bad dream. Can you please just tell them that everything in Tauronia is as it should be? And then we can all get back to bed."

Slashermite looked at Electrotaur, his finger-blades scraping together anxiously. Electrotaur looked at Slashermite and the dial on his chest went up a few notches of its own accord. He began to vibrate slightly louder and a few sparks shot off his tail and fingertips.

"Electrotaur . . . *tablecloth!*" said Aunt Thea, and the Taur quickly lifted his hands away from her nice blue tablecloth, to avoid his sparks hitting it.

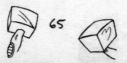

"Lady Thea," began Slashermite, "we cannot do as you ask." He looked wretched. "We cannot say all is normal in Tauronia . . . for it is not."

"Well, obviously, I don't expect Tauronia to be normal in the *normal* sense of normal," said Aunt Thea. "I mean normal in the terrifyingly *ab*normal sense that Tauronia is normally normal."

"That makes sense," said Lewis, with one eyebrow up.

"No – it is not abnormally normally normal," said Slashermite. "We have a new Taur. And we think that perhaps something is wrong with Jack or Lewis to have created such a thing. We tried to send a message to them . . . through the power of our *thoughts* . . ." Slashermite stared intently into the middle distance and waved his finger-blades to and fro in a mystic sort of way.

"So *that* was why we had the same dream!" said Jack.

"A new Taur?" said Lewis. "Oh – you mean *Flower*taur? Oh, don't worry about him. He seems sick-makingly cute but he's actually a vicious assassin."

"No, not Flowertaur," said Slashermite. "We know about him. He came along with Wuffamite. There is another."

"Another?" Jack and Lewis said together. They looked at Aunt Thea, who shook her head and held up her hands. "Not me! You know my Taurs are always useless and fall apart in minutes. I haven't bothered since my hero Taur left his leg by the standing stone. You know I'm too grown-up to make them last."

"So who is this Taur?" asked Jack, his throat feeling tight and dry.

"She is called Care-a-mite," said Slashermite. "She gives out marshmallows and wears roses around her head. She . . . *cares* . . . all the time. Without mercy."

Lewis gulped. Jack looked horrified. "She . . . *cares?*" he whispered.

"Yes," went on Slashermite. "She is impossible to stop. She has made up poems about Lavataur. She has knitted ponchos for the Dragotaurs. She tried to stick sequins to Electrotaur's shoulders. She has . . . she has . . . *made us . . . do. . ."*

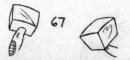

"Do what?" croaked Lewis, but Slashermite could not speak.

Electrotaur leaned forward, buzzing and humming even more intensely. "A GROUP HUG," he concluded. He sat up straight again and glared at Jack and Lewis. Something glittered prettily on his left shoulder. "WHY HAVE YOU VISITED CARE-A-MITE UPON US?"

Jack shook his head and gripped the edge of the table. He was scared now. *Really* scared.

"We didn't," he said. "Care-a-mite is nothing to do with us."

Lewis and Aunt Thea looked horrified too. "How has this happened?" murmured Aunt Thea. "How has this happened?"

"I told you," said Jack. "I told you she *knew*!"

"What – Dahlia?" said Lewis. "But how could *she* make a Taur? She hasn't got any Merrion's Mead – has she?"

"Hasn't she?" asked Jack. And he went to Aunt Thea's tall cupboards and swept down all the other bottles. They had used up one bottle (most of which had got spilled when Electrotaur and Slashermite were first brought to life) and were halfway through a second – but all the others were full. Or were they? Jack began to shake them all.

"You can't think she's been into my cupboard!" said Aunt Thea. Jack handed her the bottles. Aunt Thea looked after the Merrion's Mead. She'd had it brought all the way from Wales by taxi, to keep safe in her cupboard and measure out in tiny drops whenever they wanted to add a Taur to Tauronia or get Electrotaur and Slashermite up to play. She knew exactly how much mead should be in each bottle.

"Oh no," she murmured, shaking each bottle in turn. "It *does* seem like there is less mead in these bottles! Oh no, no, no!"

"But how could she have got in here and got it?" asked Lewis. "I mean – how?"

"I don't know." Aunt Thea bit her lip and wrinkled her brow. "I've been here most of the time – I've only been out during the day, while you've all been at school with her. So she must have got in while I was here . . . maybe while I was asleep. . ." She shuddered. "No! No I *can't* believe it. There would be a broken window or a forced lock or something." She got up and went swiftly to the window to check. Then out into the hall, into the front room, upstairs . . . to every door and window. Minutes later she was back. "No – there is *no* sign of any kind of break-in. And I haven't left any doors or windows open. It's just not possible. There *must* be some other explanation."

She sat down again, looking calmer, and took a deep breath. "You know, I think maybe there *wasn't* all that much mead in the bottles . . . I'm just imagining silly things. You probably splashed rather too much on your last drawings. And I also think that you boys *might* have somehow made up Care-a-mite . . . subconsciously. I mean, you were thinking about Dahlia and all this Play Nicely Campaign nonsense such a lot while you were drawing your new Taurs yesterday. Yes . . . yes, that's it. One of you made up Care-a-mite by mistake."

Jack and Lewis gaped at Aunt Thea. "But *how?*" said Lewis. "We didn't *draw* her, did we?"

"Look – I don't know! It's nearly three o'clock in the morning!" said Aunt Thea. "Maybe you *can* just think of something and if you're thinking of it while you're pouring mead on something else . . . maybe it can come to life without you actually drawing it or even knowing that it has! And it's more likely than a very well-behaved nine-year-old Pupil of the Month breaking in and rifling through my cupboards, now isn't it?"

Jack suddenly felt very tired. Lewis sagged next to him. It was all so worrying.

"Come on – we're all overtired and hysterical," said Aunt Thea. "Taurs back to Tauronia – boys back to sleep! I'm going to drive you both home and you must go straight to bed and in the morning we'll all be laughing about this."

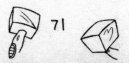

Chapter Seven

Someone Special
Idol Factor

Miss Budd stood on the school hall stage on Wednesday. Next to her was a line up of six someones who were special. Really special. So special, they had been voted for by hundreds of people.

There was Callum Wrenchnorth from year six, the best football player in the school; Billy Temple from year five, the best basketball player in school; Gillian Teeple, the best hockey player in school; Jenny Sopwith, who'd broken her arm and given everyone the chance to write on her cast while she told them the gory details; Stephen Biggs, whose dad ran a sweet shop and Dahlia Dawkins who was ... well ... Dahlia Dawkins.

"It's going to be really difficult to choose our winning Someone Special Idol," simpered Miss Budd. "They are all so very, *very* special."

Jack stared hard at Dahlia Dawkins, who stood up on the stage with an angelic smile on her face. Her golden hair was perfectly neat and her school uniform was spotless. Her shoes were free of scuffs and her badges were shiny. There was nothing about her to suggest that she was a burglar, or worse, a secret creator of disgustingly nice Taurs. No . . . he couldn't believe it. Dahlia was sick-making, of course. He would dearly love to see her fall face-first into a cow pat, but he now realized that they had all been a bit overwrought last night to imagine that Dahlia had somehow stumbled upon their secret and then stolen it. That was just silly.

"So now – the moment of truth!" said Miss Budd in a loud stage whisper. "Who will win Someone Special Idol Factor? Who will leave the stage a loser . . . and who will hold aloft this fabulous trophy?!" She picked up a small gold-coloured trophy cup and its plastic base fell off.

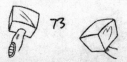

"Aaa-aaa-ahh!" marvelled the school with wonder. And sarcasm.

"You all have six cards in your hands," breathed Miss Budd. "A different colour for each of our Someone Special Idol finalists. Now it's down to *you* to choose who will win and who will leave the stage!"

Not much doubt about who would win, thought Jack. The school's best footballer was always the most popular, no question. It was like asking which day you liked best – Wednesday, Thursday, Saturday or Christmas Day? He chose the blue card in his lap and prepared to lift it up. All around him boys did the same.

Lewis picked up the yellow card, deciding to vote for Jenny Sopwith. She was in his class. He'd signed her cast and she'd told him at least three times about how the snapped bone had stuck right out through her arm. That had to be worth a vote.

"OK, everyone – get ready to vote!" gushed Miss Budd, pacing the stage like an overexcited TV presenter.

Jack lifted his card. It was easy enough

to do. Nothing in any way tricky about it. And yet, as he did so, he felt an odd tingling sensation running from his fingers, right up to his shoulder and across his neck. The hairs all stood up on his arm and head. He blinked. That was a bit odd.

On stage Miss Budd seemed to have stopped pretending she was a TV presenter. She stood still, her mouth open and her eyes round. Eventually she shook her head and said, "Goodness me." Behind her, five of the Someone Specials looked at each other with confusion and annoyance. One, however, stood still, and smiled like an angel.

"What?" spluttered Lewis when he turned his card around. He distinctly remembered picking up the yellow card for Jenny and her broken arm, and now he saw that it wasn't yellow at all. It was *pink*! Dahlia Dawkins' colour!

Jack saw Lewis across the other side of the school hall, examining the pink card with disgust. He turned his around and saw that it was not blue. It was pink. All around him murmurs of shock and disgust were growing as everyone turned their cards over and realized that they were pink.

About a quarter of the audience were smiling and beginning to clap – the girls who actually *had* voted for Dahlia.

Jack gulped. Something was wrong here. Something was very wrong.

"Well – I can't quite believe it! But we have a clear – very clear – winner!" said Miss Budd in a high-pitched voice. "Dahlia Dawkins!"

Dahlia skipped forward to receive the gold- coloured cup, taking care to hold its base on. "Thank you! Thank you *all*. . ." she said. "Truly – I don't know what to say . . . except *everyone* on the stage today is special – and everyone in the audience is special. Very, very special! With a specialness which is a especially special to me . . . your Someone Special Idol. . ."

It seemed to Lewis that Dahlia's triumphant smile flashed directly at Jack, who was sitting down, looking aghast, the pink card still trembling in his hand. The audience was muttering and getting restless but now Miss Stretch, the head teacher, strode on to the stage and everyone quietened down.

"Well – what a lovely speech, Dahlia," said Miss Stretch. "And I'm sure your award is well deserved, especially for all the wonderful positive games you have brought to the playground this week. I've rarely seen our school behaving so nicely."

"May I just say," butted in Dahlia. "That it's nice to be important, but it's important to be nice." Her collection of genuine girl voters clapped and cheered and Miss Stretch patted Dahlia on the head.

"As our Someone Special Idol, you're allowed to choose what the school does for the rest of the day," said Miss Stretch. The whole school held its breath. . . Art? Games? Drama? A film in the hall? All of these things were a possibility.

"Well, I would like to choose mathematics," said Dahlia. "As I'm sure we would all benefit very much from it . . . but as everyone has been so kind to me, I think we should probably all go out for nice play – with the PNC in charge."

Half the audience cheered and the other half groaned and muttered.

"I have new wool!" promised Dahlia. "We can finger-knit for starving orphans. . ."

As the school filed out of the hall, Lewis walked past the front of stage where Dahlia and the five runners-up still waited. Dahlia was *kissing* each of them on the cheek, despite the disgusted protests from the boys. As she bent to slurp against Callum's horrified face, a screwed-up bit of paper fell from the sleeve of her spotless white blouse and rolled to the edge of the stage. Lewis grabbed it quickly and stuffed it in his own pocket, prickles of dread running up and down his spine.

"Help . . . me . . ." whimpered Billy Temple to Lewis, but it was too late for him, as Dahlia swooped down and planted one on his frozen grimace. Lewis looked away. It might be too late for *all* of them if his awful fear proved to be true.

As soon as he got outside, he found Jack waiting for him. Lewis pulled the screwed-up bit of paper out of his pocket and flattened it out against the playground wall. They both stared at it in horror. It was a picture of rows and rows of children in an audience. Every single one of them was holding up a card. A pink card. Jack sniffed the paper and nodded grimly at Lewis.

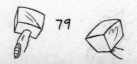

The honey scent of mead was still on it.

"It's true," murmured Jack, going pale. "She really *has* stolen the mead. But how?"

"Doesn't matter *how* any more," said Lewis. "This is big trouble. She hasn't got an Aunt Thea to remind her about the dangers. She's already using it in the real world! She's just ripped a hole in the fabric of time, space and reality."

"You what?" said Jack.

Lewis shrugged. "Well . . . you know. That kind of thing."

"Yeah," agreed Jack. "She's messed with everyone's minds, that's for sure. Mind you – she was doing that even without the mead!"

"What are we going to do?" Lewis stared across the playground to the group of girls and a few boys, all concentrating on looping wool around their fingers, with Dahlia at their centre. "We've got to get the magic mead off her and stop all this! What if she meads *us* into always playing nicely and joining in the finger-knitting?"

Jack gulped. "We have to get to Aunt Thea

and draw ourselves Dahlia-resistant cloaks or helmets or something. Then we've got to find the stolen mead and get it back . . . then we've got to get Slashermite to do a *proper* hypnotism on Dahlia. If we *don't* . . ." He took a deep breath. "If we *don't* . . . we might wake up tomorrow morning in DAHLIAWORLD."

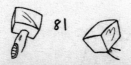

Chapter Eight

Breaking Rules

"Anti-Dahlia helmets," said Lewis. "That's what we need. Full of Dahlianite. The only known substance which can fend off a Dahlia attack."

He and Jack hurried through the woods, their school backpacks bashing against their shoulders as they leaped over the little stream and ran up the bank on the other side. They hadn't even gone home first – they had to get straight to Aunt Thea's. Their mum would probably tell them off for not going coming back and getting out of their school clothes . . . but this couldn't wait.

"What if we're too late?" puffed Jack, as they ran along the stepping stones and across the river. Clouds were rolling in low and the sky was dark and ominous, like their mood. "Dahlia could have made it back home before us, and could be making a picture about *us* right now. She could be about to mead us at any second, and turn us into Little Fairy Tippytoes and the Cuddly Pink Pixie!"

Aunt Thea was not in when they got to her cottage, but Jack found the key hidden under Tibbles, the dog-shaped stone in her rockery, and let them both in.

"We're breaking her rule," said Lewis, as Jack reached up to the high shelf in the cupboard to get the Merrion's Mead. "She said we must never, ever mead anything without her being here."

He and Jack looked at each other solemnly. They didn't normally break promises. "This is an emergency," said Jack. "She'll understand."

They grabbed some paper and crayons from the drawer in the big kitchen table and swiftly drew the Anti-Dahlia helmets. At first they made them big and shiny and Lewis put horns on his – with blood dripping off the tips – and then Jack stopped him. "Look – we need to be

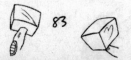 83

wearing these at school!" he said. "They've got to look the part."

And so, with a shudder, Jack redesigned his Anti-Dahlia helmet. Lewis copied him with a grimace, also making his look just like the neat green schoolboy caps which hardly any boy at their school ever wore. You could buy them from the school's reception and some of the mums occasionally did, thinking they looked "cute". What these mothers failed to realize was that wearing a school cap was exactly like wearing a cardboard crown, with the words "PLEASE KICK ME – I'M A DWEEB" on it. Any boy dim enough to proudly wear his cap into school had usually somehow "lost" it before a week was out. The backs of radiators at Shawley Junior were stuffed with barely worn school caps. The high tops of the lockers, unseen by anyone but the caretaker when he got up on a ladder to change light bulbs, were a school cap graveyard. The caretaker never attempted to get the caps down and give them back to their owners. He understood the ways of boys.

But tomorrow Jack and Lewis would wear

school caps. All day. No matter what. What's more, they would even take some spares and try to convince their friends to wear them too. If it wasn't too late.

"OK – I've made four caps," said Lewis.

"Me too," said Jack. "But we can't make them real here – that's *really* going to upset Aunt Thea. Let's draw them at the bottom of the steps down into Tauronia. Then we can get Electrotaur and Slashermite to bring them up for us. I want to check on them anyway – find out what Care-a-mite is getting up to."

"Shouldn't we wait for Aunt Thea?" asked Lewis anxiously.

"We can't wait," said Jack. "Dahlia could use the mead again at any moment. Come on – spill!"

They both dripped a little mead on to their drawings of Electrotaur and Slashermite exiting the standing stone, carrying their Anti-Dahlia caps, and then raced up the garden to meet them. At the doorway in the standing stone they met their Taurs, who were both, as drawn,

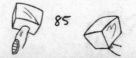

carrying Shawley Junior school caps, two in
each hand.

"Thanks, Slashy," said Lewis. "Sorry – we
can't invite you in because Aunt Thea's not
here and we haven't really got permission even
to get you up out of Tauronia."

Slashermite handed Lewis his caps. He
didn't say anything. Nor did Electrotaur, as he

passed four caps to Jack. This was not unusual for Electrotaur. He wasn't much of a talker – but Slashermite was rarely quiet. "What's up, you two?" asked Jack, suddenly worried.

"All is not well," sighed Slashermite. "All is not well *at all* in Tauronia."

"What? What's happened?" demanded Lewis.

"It is hard to explain," said Slashermite, his bright eyes cast down and his finger-blades meekly tucked in. "You have to be there."

Jack and Lewis looked at each other and then at the doorway to Tauronia. Of all the things they were *most* forbidden to do, going down to Tauronia was the most forbidden of all.

"We'll just have a peep," said Jack. "We're in trouble anyway. . ."

Aunt Thea walked briskly back from shops. As she turned the corner into River Lane she was met with a blue flashing light and a gathering of neighbours, talking together in hushed tones beside a police car.

"What's going on?" she asked Mrs Peebles.

The old lady tugged her cardigan tight across

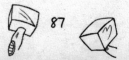

her chest and shook her head. "Oh! You wouldn't believe it! Gracie Lewis has been burgled! All her silverware! Gone! In the night!"

"No!" Aunt Thea squinted up the pathway of the little cottage – the very last one on their row of terraced homes. "Is she OK?"

"She's having a turn, I should say," said Mrs Peebles. "She could've been murdered in her bed."

Aunt Thea nodded sympathetically.

"She could've had her head bashed in with a rusty pole."

"Mmmm," said Aunt Thea, watching a uniformed policeman walking up the path to the end cottage, speaking into his walkie-talkie.

"She could have had her arms broken with a wooden club."

"Yes, Mrs Peebles."

"She could've had her legs smashed with a cricket bat. . ."

"You really must meet my nephews some time," suggested Aunt Thea. "You'd all get on so well." She went to walk on but Mrs Peebles grabbed her elbow.

 88

"Just you watch out, Miss Casterbridge! They're saying number 12's been done as well. We've been *targeted* – all of us!" Her neighbours gathered closer together in a worried knot. "I shall be afraid to go to sleep! They come in the night, silent as the grave, with their cricket bats and their rusty poles . . . and you never even know they've been! Not a sound. Not a thing out of place. . ."

"Sounds like my kind of burglar," said Aunt Thea brightly. "Quiet – and cleans up after himself."

The neighbours gave her a hard stare.

At the foot of the stone steps, Jack and Lewis drank in the view of Tauronia. Jack felt a thrill of excitement and fear run through him. Tauronia was just so fantastic.

A wide valley meandered between mountains and volcanoes, with a river curling through it and flowing out to the Tauronian Sea, where Noodlemite Eels swam in huge shoals, like ocean spaghetti, and Aquataur took favoured guests on little jaunts under the sea by the volcanic outflows

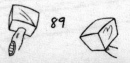

where it was warm and fizzy. Castles of all kinds were dotted around the mountains, including the jewel-encrusted home of Electrotaur and Slashermite. Dragotaurs chased tiny colourful Aviamites across the turquoise sky above them.

"Looks pretty fab to me!" said Lewis, also taking in the view with great pride. Although he and Jack had made up Tauronia in their minds for years, they had brought it all to life with their drawings and the magic mead some months ago, just for Electrotaur and Slashermite to live in. Almost every week they added a new bit to it. Lewis was particularly

pleased with his railway, which had begun a regular Millipedataur service only last month. Ten huge Millipedataurs now ran along the track, each arriving at Tauronia Halt every five minutes, for an express journey to the Molten Swamps of Badcurry or the Boffinataurs' Castle or the seaside. The only problem was that Millipedataurs were all rather smooth and shiny and you had to really concentrate not to fall off their curved brown backs while their hundreds of pairs of legs pounded along the track. He really must put some proper seats on them, thought Lewis.

"Come with us," said Slashermite. "We will show you."

They led their creators swiftly down the slope towards the Tauronian town square. In the centre, around a slightly nibbled chocolate statue of Jack and Lewis, was a crowd of Taurs – most of them sitting in fold-out camping chairs. There must be at least fifty, thought Jack, marvelling at the weird and wonderful collection of creatures. He could see Lavataur, clapping his pumice-stone hands and slowly burning through his metal folding stool, as his molten body glowed and crisped up slightly at the edges. Nobody was sitting too close to him. Stinkermite was there too, in a nice yellow mini dress and high-heeled boots, dribbling pink goo down his chest. Tundrataur, Scale-a-taur, Dismembamite, Bouldermite, Mechanitaur, Shockermite – and even Grippakillataur was there, Jack saw, with a stab of fear. The last time they'd met *him*, he'd crushed Electrotaur's arm and very nearly eaten their cousin. Jack remembered exactly why coming down here was quite a bad idea.

But there was no need to worry today.

Everyone was sitting around, waving and whooping and *clapping*! In front of them, using the lower part of the chocolate fudge plinth of Jack and Lewis's statue as a stage, was what could only be Care-a-mite. The sign behind her was the clue. It said "CARE-A-MITE'S CARING SHOW – LET'S ALL CARE!"

Chapter Nine

The Ugly Hug Ball

Care-a-mite wore a long, golden, sequined dress over her plump curvy form, glittery ruby shoes on her feet and white roses all around her head. Her skin was a velvety pale pink material. She had a sweet, sympathetic smile, two bright violet eyes and a little snub nose. Her hair, flowing out from under the roses, was yellow and finger-knitted. She was carrying a basket filled

with pink and white marshmallows, which she threw out to the audience from time to time. Heaps of marshmallows lay in their laps and everyone was scoffing them as fast as they were whooping . . . which was leading to the occasional choking situation.

In spite of his anxiety, Slashermite dug his hands into a marshmallow drift and stood up with two or three squishy sugar pillows on every finger-blade. He sucked them into his mouth, a bladeful at a time, as they found some spare seats next to Wuffamite and sat down, taking great care not to touch Wuffamite's tail.

Next to Care-a-mite on the stage was a big Taur, sitting on a fold-out stool. Jack vaguely recognized him. He screwed up his eyes and then put on his glasses.

"You know . . . I *know* that you care. Deeply. We *all* can see that here today. Even though you don't show it," Care-a-mite said, up on her stage, and she rested her velvety pink hand on the Taur's robust purple shoulder. Cautiously. There were some pretty nasty spikes there.

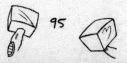

The audience whooped and shouted things like "Yeah!" and "You care, Taur! You *care!*"

"So, tell us your story. We're all here for you today . . . tell us your story."

"Stor-y! Stor-y! Stor-y!" chanted the audience, until Care-a-mite put up her hand and called for quiet.

"It's just that . . ." the Taur sniffed, "I feel like I'm invisible."

"No," said Care-a-mite sweetly. "*He's* invisible. . ." And she pointed to another chair with two blue eyeballs floating three feet above it. There was a slightly embarrassed rustling noise and the eyes swivelled down towards the creature's invisible feet. Invisitaur – one of their aunt's few unreliable creations – was obviously a second guest on the Care-a-mite Show.

"You are the one with *relationship* issues," reminded Care-a-mite, patting the Taur carefully on the shoulder again.

"Oh – yeah – sorry." The Taur sat up straight and then glared at the audience. "So what's it to you? Eh? So – I got issues! So what?"

"I feel your anger," sighed Care-a-mite. "We all do. And we all care. . ."

"My son doesn't even know who I am," said the Taur, his tough voice suddenly breaking into a sob. "He doesn't seem to know I exist."

"Well – that's where you're wrong, Slashertaur!" cried Care-a-mite. "Because we've found your son and he's here TODAY!" The audience erupted into whoops and squeals and that vague familiarity suddenly made sense to Jack. Oh no! Before he could say anything, poor Slashermite was swept up by Wuffamite and borne up to the stage, his little purple legs pistoning into the air in shock.

"Slashermite – it's time you met your dad – Slashertaur!" The audience was screaming with delight and several creatures were mopping away tears as Slashermite stood on the stage, bewildered. Jack felt very bad. Of course . . . Slashertaur was one of the first Taurs he had ever created! And he'd forgotten completely to mention him to Slashermite – even though he was his father! Jack and Lewis had found a collection of early Taur drawings some months

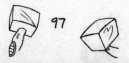

ago, soon after Tauronia was created, and had quickly meaded the lot of them, to help fill up their new land. He'd never thought to let Slashermite know about his father . . . he'd just forgotten. Lewis had forgotten, too.

Looking at Slashertaur you could tell he was an early Taur . . . he wasn't quite so well drawn. He had the same purple colouring as Slashermite and of course, being a Taur, he was a lot bigger, with a more fearsome rhino horn and a couple of rather odd-looking, stunted wings with more spikes on. His finger-blades were much shorter though, and quite clumpy. Which was probably just as well, as he was reaching for his son now, and hadn't thought to tuck the blades out of the way.

"My boy! My boy!" sniffed Slashertaur.

"Hug! Hug! Hug! Hug!" demanded the crowd. Slashermite stood next to Care-a-mite, who was now looking from father to son with a drippy expression on her face, holding one of their hands in each of hers.

Slashermite stared across at Lewis and Jack, a look of horror and embarrassment on his face.

Prodded by Care-a-mite he stumbled across to Slashertaur who stood up, fully seven foot tall, and held open his purple arms.

Awkwardly, Slashermite gave a watery grin and shuffled into his surprised father's embrace.

"Aaaawwwww!" went the audience and Grippakillataur picked up a nearby woolly Mite and wiped his many little eyes with it, oblivious to the screams and wriggling.

"So – Slashermite! You've met your dad! For the first time!" breathed Care-o-mite, pulling him out of the uncomfortable hug and putting her arm around his shoulders.

"How do you feel? Thrilled? Crushed? Angry? Confused?"

"Sick," said Slashermite, and threw up on her ruby shoes.

It was all the marshmallows of course. Or else it was the whole Care-a-mite's Caring Show thing, which certainly made Jack feel sick, and he hadn't eaten any marshmallows at all.

For a moment the smile on Care-a-mite's face twitched as she surveyed the mess trickling into her shoes. The audience gasped. Then two

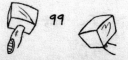

99

small Mites ran over with a bucket and a mop and cleaned Care-a-mite's sticky feet.

"Well . . . I can see that you're really overwhelmed with joy, Slashermite," said Care-a-mite. "Maybe you need to hug your daddy again!" The audience murmured, "Hug! Hug!" in a slightly less enthusiastic way this time and, as Slashermite ambled towards Slashertaur, with sticky gloops of already-eaten marshmallow dripping off his chin, Slashertaur backed away.

"Brilliant to see you, son . . . we must catch up again, sometime soon. . ." gulped Slashertaur. His stubby wings began to beat wildly and he rose up like a helicopter, out of gloopy, sticky harm's way. "Laters!" he added and was gone.

Care-a-mite faced the audience and sighed, her head tilted to one side. "And that's the sad face of abandonment . . . seen so often in Tauronia today. Poor Slashermite – to have the joy of at last meeting his father, only to lose him again three minutes later! No . . . don't cry, Slashermite." Slashermite gave her a sarcastic look.

"Be strong . . . for me . . ." she continued. "And for every Mite that's lost its Taur . . . perhaps for ever. . . Tauronians – we should learn to *care* about each other, even when our fathers abandon us." Care-a-mite smiled winningly at the crowd and added: "I'm Care-a-mite – you've been a fantastic audience! Goodnight!"

To cheers and squeaks and bellows and chants of "Care-y, Care-y, Care-y!" she ran from the stage and disappeared into a nearby house.

Jack and Lewis looked at each other, aghast. How could this be happening in the world they had created? All around them their Taurs and Mites were getting up, folding their chairs and ambling off. They went with Electrotaur to collect Slashermite, who was sitting down on the edge of the stage, looking rather appalled.

"Slashy, we're sorry," said Lewis. "We should have said about you having a dad. We just forgot."

"He wasn't . . . very well drawn," said Slashermite.

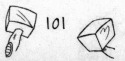

"No," admitted Jack. "Lewis did a much better job of you."

"Cheer up," said Lewis, pulling Slashermite up by his shiny purple wrist. "We've seen enough. We know who's done this. We're going to put a stop to it."

Jack eyed the door of the house Care-a-mite had disappeared into. "Right," he said. "Wait here, all of you. I'm going to talk to Care-a-mite and find out what happened."

He strode across to the house, which had a pink door with more roses climbing around it and those frilly gathered-up curtains at its windows. He knocked once and then pushed open the door.

Care-a-mite stood arranging flowers at a table. She gave him a treacly smile. "You must be Jack," she said. "I recognize you from your statue. I hope you're thoroughly ashamed of yourself."

"You what?" spluttered Jack.

"For creating all these violent, negative characters to live in Tauronia."

"Now wait just a minute!" said Jack. "I can put whatever characters I like into

Tauronia! So can Lewis! We created it! And anyway – what I want to know is what the heck *you're* doing here! We didn't draw you! Or mead you. So who did? Dahlia, I bet!"

Care-a-mite smirked. "Just as well, too, don't you think? Tauronia is in a terrible state. I am here to put it right and make everyone play nicely."

"Oh no you don't!" growled Jack and then he blinked. "How did Dahlia even know how to get you here? And what it looked like? And what was going on down here?"

"Oh that was easy – she's got your drawings. She took them out of Lewis's bag at school. She saw them when she was putting finger-knitting wool in. She only did it to help you give up your

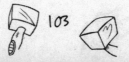

nasty school games, but when she stumbled in on you and your Taurs and then read about the magic mead in your Tauronia folder all she had to do was go through your drawings to work out exactly what dreadful things you were up to. And she then made me, so I can put everything right!"

"How did she get the mead? She's a thief!" shouted Jack.

"She's a saviour," sighed Care-a-mite. "And so am I. Am I not wonderful?"

"You're horrifying," said Jack. "And you don't belong here. We'll get you out! See if we don't. Why did you have to come down here? Why can't you just stay with Dahlia?"

"Well, I can visit Dahlia, like Electrotaur and Slashermite visit you – but we both know that I can't *stay* in the Overworld all the time. And besides – I'm needed here! You'll see. I will make everything love-leeee. Marshmallow?"

"We'll stop you!" warned Jack.

"Try it," smiled Care-a-mite. "Just remember, you're not the only one with magic mead now. . ."

Jack shuddered and went back outside. He

found Lewis, Electrotaur and Slashermite at the foot of the path that led back to the Overworld. He told them about what he'd learned from Care-a-mite.

"We can draw her into a sealed underground vault and leave her there," muttered Lewis.

"No, we can't. We can't make her go in! We can't control Taurs or Mites we haven't made ourselves. Remember? Only *Dahlia* can control Care-a-mite now."

"OK – let's get Grippakillataur to eat her," said Lewis.

"No," said Jack. "If she got away and told Dahlia, I bet Dahlia would do something awful with the mead she's nicked."

"Right, so we get Slashy to hypnotize Dahlia, properly, like we said!" replied Lewis, as they waved goodbye to Electrotaur and Slashermite and climbed back up the spiral stone steps. "Then we get our pictures back and then get the mead back and. . ."

"OK – but how do we get Slashy in front of her? We only see her at school. And she'll know not to look at him – she knows all about

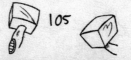

105

his powers. She's got the Tauronia folder. She knows *everything*!"

"I'm really sorry, Jack," said Lewis. He stared miserably at his shoes. If he hadn't been showing off to Henry, none of this could have happened.

"I know," said Jack. "We'll work it out. But first we have to tell Aunt Thea where we've been. She's not going to like it."

They were right about that.

"I don't care *what* Electrotaur and Slashermite told you!" said Aunt Thea. "I can't believe you would be so irresponsible, Jack, to take your little brother back down there, *knowing* how dangerous it is!"

"But we had to," protested Lewis, while Jack felt very uncomfortable. Aunt Thea was right – he *should* protect his little brother.

"We couldn't just let them go back on their own and not find out what was going on!" went on Lewis.

"Oh yes, you could!" retorted Aunt Thea. "Slashermite is perfectly able to describe what's happening. I shall be having words with him, too –

that's if either of them ever come up to Overworld again. I tell you, it's too dangerous. I am seriously thinking of pouring all the mead down the sink."

"No!" shouted Jack and Lewis together.

"We'll never be able to defeat Dahlia if we haven't got any mead!" said Jack. "She'll be the only one who's got it and knows what it can do! Care-a-mite told me Dahlia stole our folder out of Lewis's bag, so she knows everything about Tauronia. That's why she sent Care-a-mite down there, to mess with our fun and make it all 'nice'. If we can't fight back she could do terrible things to it! And worse than that – she's using magic mead outside Tauronia. She wants to control the whole school! If we don't stop her the whole planet will turn into Dahliaworld."

Aunt Thea pressed her lips together and looked at them. She had to admit their story was very, very worrying. Then there was a knock at the door and someone shouted, "Yoohoo! Thea! Have you got Jack and Lewis?"

It was their mum! Jack and Lewis looked stricken. They hadn't even phoned to say where they were.

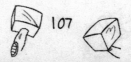

The telling off they got was as much as they deserved. Their mum had been very worried and Aunt Thea gave them very dark looks throughout.

"Are you still coming into school tomorrow?" asked Lewis, forlornly, as Mum went ahead with Jack, still telling him off, and getting him into the car. "Remember . . . it's Someone Special visitors day."

"Yes, Lewis – I'll be there," sighed Aunt Thea. "And I may have worked out something else about the Dawkins – something which might help solve our problem. We'll talk again tomorrow."

"Yes," mumbled Lewis, and they shuffled off down the path feeling dejected. Everything was going wrong. But at least the Anti-Dahlia caps were stuffed securely into his and Jack's pockets.

When they had gone, Aunt Thea walked upstairs and stood on the landing. She looked up at the ceiling for some time. Then she narrowed her eyes and nodded. "Oh yes," she said. "*Now* I get it!"

Chapter Ten

Join On

Everyone was wearing friendship bracelets at school. They were finger-knitted, of course, but quite a few had beads and sequins in them too. The finger-knitting group now covered half the playground and had become a kind of friendship-bracelet factory. Tendrils of wool trailed off it. It was as if a vast, pulsating, smiling Martian plant had taken root at Shawley Junior.

When one of Jack's regular bullies came up and insisted he put a bracelet on, he knew for sure that Dahlia was using Merrion's Mead in the real world again, so she could take control and rule the playground.

"Baz . . . I don't *want* a friendship bracelet," said Jack. "Stop being such a noobstick!" He

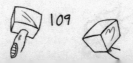

109

took off his glasses, to save them from being broken when Baz smacked his face in.

But Baz didn't smack his face in. He pouted. "I *made* this for you!" he said in a hurt voice, waving the purple and yellow woolly bangle, with two heart-shaped beads woven into it.

"Baz! Why would you want to make a friendship bracelet for me? You're my bully – not my friend! You don't want to put anything round my wrist except a Chinese burn! What's *wrong* with you?" Jack held his breath and waited for the punch which *must* come now, surely.

It didn't. Baz sniffed and turned on his heel. "You're so negative! I'm never speaking to you again!" he huffed as he flounced away. Jack stared in horror as, a few seconds later, Baz began to canter on an imaginary horse, kicking up his heels and making high-pitched neighing noises, before rejoining the finger-knitting collective.

In the middle of all this, Dahlia sat like a queen, sending her minions out to force friendship bracelets on the few children left who weren't already in her gang. Jack pulled

his cap down tighter on his head and watched, sadly, as Kevin crossed the playground, arm in arm with Kirsty, whispering and giggling. Kevin had refused to wear the Dahlia-proof cap. He hadn't believed what Jack had told him and now he had been brainwashed too.

"It's not looking good, is it?" Lewis stepped around the large oak tree at the perimeter of the playground and tapped Jack on the shoulder. "I couldn't get any of my mates to wear the caps either."

"Who's that then?" asked Jack. A figure, some way off, was definitely wearing a cap. He squinted. "Is that a girl?"

"Yeah – one in your class, I think," said Lewis.

"Sarah Adams," said Jack. "Blimey! She must have found the one Kevin threw away. She's probably going to stick love beads all over it. Oh no – now what are they doing?"

Dahlia's lackeys were suddenly forming into a great big chain, holding hands. They were chanting. They were moving around the playground, gathering speed, like a human fishnet. "Join on, join on," they chanted,

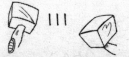 111

"if you want to play. Join on, join on, if you want to play. . ." Anyone who didn't join on was enclosed by the net anyway. Friendship bracelets were put on, despite struggles . . . and then the struggles stopped and the new "friend" simply "joined on".

"Quick!" said Lewis. "Up the tree!"

He and Jack were quite good climbers, having spent so much time playing in the woods, and they scrambled up the tree before the chain reached their end of the playground. It swept on past below them, chanting, but nobody looked up. Nobody looked anywhere, really. They just smiled and smiled and smiled. . .

"Help me!" hissed a voice and Jack looked down, startled. "Quick – help me get up before they come round again!" He stared, amazed. It was Sarah Adams. She was, indeed, wearing one of the Dahlia-proof caps and struggling to get up the thick trunk of the tree.

"What if it's a trick?" said Lewis, but Jack anchored his feet around his branch and swung down to haul Sarah up. She grabbed his hands and scrabbled her shiny black shoes against the

 112

trunk, and eventually got up on the branches next to them, puffing.

"How come you're not down there – with your beloved Dahlia?" asked Lewis.

"She's *not* my beloved anything!" said Sarah. "Why do you think I've got the cap on?"

"How do you know about the caps?" asked Jack uneasily. "Have you been spying on us for Dahlia?"

"Yes, of course I've been spying on you," said Sarah. "But not for Dahlia. Although *Dahlia*

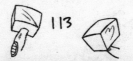

thinks I'm spying for Dahlia, obviously." She tucked a bit of fair hair tightly under the cap and looked at them both, solemnly. "This time last week, I *would* have been spying for her. I would have done anything for her. But not any more. She's mad. She's completely mad. She wants everyone to worship her. Well, she's not making *me*!"

"So . . . you're on *our* side?" marvelled Jack.

"I was never on anyone's side before. I didn't think there were sides. Just people, being people. I agreed with her that you were disgusting with all your gory games – but I never expected her to really stop you and make you play only her games. It doesn't seem right. People should be allowed to play their own games. If only Dahlia's fun is allowed, it's not really fun any more."

"You got *that* right!" said Lewis.

"So – I was spying on you. And I heard you talking to Kevin about the caps. And how if you wore one, Dahlia wouldn't be able to brainwash you. And I wouldn't have believed it – but I saw what she did yesterday in Someone Special Idol Factor. And that was brainwashing, wasn't

114

it? And I didn't want to be next. So I found Kevin's cap and put it on. I don't know how it works, but I haven't been brainwashed yet. And I don't think she's noticed."

"Hasn't she?" said Jack.

Sarah and Lewis followed his gaze. Down at the foot of the tree, staring up at them, surrounded by a sea of silent, smiling admirers, stood Dahlia Dawkins.

"Join on," said Dahlia.

"Morning, Doris!" called out Aunt Thea cheerily, as she went down her garden path with a bag of curiosities to take to Shawley Junior School.

Doris gave her a stiff nod and shut her front door behind her. She too was carrying a bag of what appeared to be a lot of knitted squares.

"Going in for Someone Special Day?" asked Aunt Thea as she unlocked the Beetle.

"Yes, of course," said Doris, as she made her way to her own car. "Are you?" She looked disdainful.

"Absolutely," grinned Aunt Thea. "I'll see you

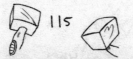

there." As she got into the car she muttered, "I can't *wait* to see you there, Doris. In just about an hour. But first. . ." Aunt Thea took out her mobile phone and dialled a number. "Is that Inspector Ross? Are you investigating the River Lane cottage burglaries? I think I may be able to help. . ."

". . .if you want to play," added Dahlia. A sea of madly smiling faces swayed below them. Feeling rather sick, Lewis noticed Henry and William and Ben among them. They must have had the bracelets forced on them. "Join on," murmured the sea. "Join on, if you want to play."

"We don't *want* to join on, Dahlia – and we don't want to play," shouted Jack. "We know what you've been up to! We're going to put a stop to it! Just you wait and see!"

Dahlia just smiled even more and narrowed her eyes up at them. "I see you've got a traitor with you. Really, Sarah – after everything you said about playing nicely! And to think I made you that friendship bracelet and you're not even wearing it."

"I'm not your friend any more. You're mad!"

shouted down Sarah, rather bravely, thought Jack, considering she was now the only girl in the whole school who had turned against Dahlia.

"You'll be sorry you didn't join us. You'll be sorry," smiled Dahlia.

"I'm not afraid of you!" shouted back Sarah. "And I *hate* finger-knitting! I'd rather pick chewing gum off the pavement."

"If you're not afraid . . . why are you all up that tree?" asked Dahlia. Jack shivered. He *was* afraid, even if he wasn't going to admit it.

Then the school bell rang, and everyone in the smiling, murmuring sea below them suddenly turned and walked obediently towards the school entrance, like good little girls and boys.

Jack, Lewis and Sarah sighed with relief and stared at each other.

"What now?" said Sarah. "We've got to go in to class and they might get us then."

"I don't think they will," said Jack. "It would be misbehaviour, during class time."

"I think we should go in late," said Lewis. "They'll all be going straight into Someone Special assembly in about five minutes – and if

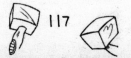

we're late back in we'll have to stand up at the side near the teachers. It'll be safer."

"We'll be in trouble," said Sarah.

"Do you care?" asked Jack and she shook her head.

"When did you decide to turn against Dahlia?" asked Lewis.

"To be honest," said Sarah. "I've never really liked her that much."

"So why were you always hanging around with her?" demanded Jack.

"Because everyone else liked her," said Sarah. "I know it's stupid, but *she* made friends with *me* – and because all the other girls said she was great, I didn't want to be left out."

"Even though you didn't like her?" said Jack, shaking his head.

"Well, yeah, she's a bit mean about people behind their backs," said Sarah. "I don't like that about her."

Lewis snorted. "She's also a dictator who brainwashes entire schools! I don't like *that* about her."

The playground was now empty. Jack checked

his watch. "OK – they should be in assembly now. Let's go. And remember, keep the hats on."

"What have you done to these hats, to make them Dahlia-proof?" asked Sarah as she climbed back down the tree.

Lewis glanced at Jack and Jack shrugged. "She'll never believe you anyway," he said.

"Well," said Lewis. "We have some magic mead, and we drew these caps to be Dahlia-proof and spilled the mead on them to make them real."

"O. . .K. . ." said Sarah as she jumped back down to the ground.

"It really is magic mead. It makes stuff come to life," explained Jack. "Dahlia found out about the mead because she stole our folder of Tauronia drawings – and then she saw two of the monsters we made with it so she knew it was true. So she stole some of our mead."

Lewis pulled out a crumpled piece of paper. "You know she made everyone vote for her yesterday? This is how she did it. She drew it – and she meaded it – see!" Lewis showed Sarah Dahlia's picture of rows and rows of children

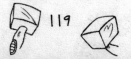

holding up pink voting cards.

Sarah stared at it and then up at Jack and Lewis. "You make monsters?" she asked.

"Yep – we call them Taurs," said Jack. "They live in Tauronia – an underground world we've created where it's safe to keep them. But Dahlia's messed around in Tauronia too. She's made a revolting Taur called Care-a-mite and Care-a-mite is trying to brainwash our Taurs too, just like Dahlia's doing here. Dahlia has to be stopped."

Sarah nodded. "Tell me what I can do to help." She linked arms with Jack and Lewis as they walked towards the school door, and although the boys pulled faces at each other, they didn't unlink. Sarah was turning out to be OK.

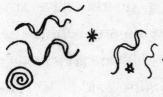

Chapter Eleven

Aunt Thea Opens Her Heart

They were told off for misbehaving and they were glad. At least they knew they still *could* misbehave.

"Sarah – I'm surprised at you," said Miss White as they shuffled into the school hall and along the side area where the teachers sat, and stood up against the wall. All the rest of the children were sitting cross-legged on the floor, their backs ramrod straight, watching the stage area. Not one of them was sprawling sideways, whispering to a mate or picking at their shoes, a scab or a nose. Every child's hands were folded neatly in their lap. Every child's face wore an expression of rapt attention and joy. Sort of. To Jack, they looked like they were all wearing

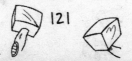

identical wax masks. Up on the stage stood Miss Budd and Miss Stretch and behind them were eight grown-ups who had been persuaded to come into the assembly as "Someone Special". Among them were Aunt Thea and Doris Dawkins, sitting at either end of the row of guests. All of the grown-ups looked rather nervous and now that he looked around him, Jack noticed that the teachers were all looking at each other uneasily too. They knew that this perfect behaviour was odd. Very odd.

Up on the stage Aunt Thea was scrutinizing the audience, looking for Jack and Lewis and as soon as she spotted them, off to the side, she grimaced at them as if to say, "What on *earth* is going on?"

Jack pointed to Dahlia and mouthed "Dahlia!" Aunt Thea nodded slowly and glanced across at Doris. Then she looked at her watch and smiled to herself.

Lewis took another rolled-up school cap out of his pocket. "We've got to get this on to Aunt Thea's head," he whispered. "Dahlia might start to brainwash the grown-ups too, at any time!"

Up on stage Miss Stretch coughed politely and began to address the audience.

"Good morning, children," she said. Normally what followed was a kind of heavy lolloping chant of "Good mo-or-ning Mi-iss Stre-etch-ch-ch-ch'. Today, however, the children came right back at her with a swift, loud and cheery "Good morning, Miss Stretch!"

Miss Stretch blinked with shock and coughed again.

"I'm – er – delighted to have on the stage with me a few of the many Someone Specials you have told us about this week. I'd like to ask each of you who has nominated one of our guests to come up on the stage and say a few words about them."

"Yesss!" said Jack, pushing Lewis forwards. "Go!"

Lewis hurtled up to the stage, shoving Dahlia out of the way – to a gasp of disapproval from all of the children watching. He ran to hug his aunt, whispering, "Quick – put this cap on. It's Dahlia-proof. She's brainwashed every single kid except me, Jack and Sarah. It might just be

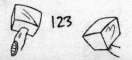

123

the bracelets, but we're not sure."

Aunt Thea hurriedly put on the cap. "Be ready for some action," she murmured back, before Lewis lined up with the other children. The children all spoke lovingly about their Someone Specials.

"My daddy is the best daddy in the world," said Kirsty. "He goes to work every day to earn money to buy me food and drink and dollies and I *wuv* him very much!" As she cuddled her slightly-abashed looking father, all the children in the audience, at exactly the same moment, tipped their heads to one side and went *Aaaaaaaaw!* Jack felt Sarah grip his arm. He gulped. This was giving him chills.

"My Someone Special is my Uncle Bob," said Baz, the ex-bully. "He taught me how to spit proper." *Aaaaaaaaaw*, went all the head-tilting children.

Jack distinctly heard Miss White mutter, "OK, now I am officially freaking out."

Lewis was second to last, before Dahlia. Nervously he stood and faced the sea of smiling masks. "M-my Aunt Thea is my Someone

Special because. . ." he began.

"You should have joined on," whispered Dahlia to his left.

"Um . . . my Aunt. . ."

"You'll be sorreee," sang Dahlia softly, "when my Someone Special arrives." Her hand was in her school skirt pocket and he heard a crinkly noise of paper. A shiver ran over him. This felt very, very bad.

"My aunt is someone special because she – she . . . makes us hot chocolate," finished Lewis lamely, staring at Dahlia's pocket with fear gripping his throat.

Aaaaaaaw! went the head-tilting children.

Now it was Dahlia's turn. She stepped to the front of the stage and raised her arms aloft. "Someone special!" she sang out. "Someone . . . special! Well, as the person that you have all voted as *your* Someone Special, it seems right that I am saved until last, here today, to talk about my very *own* Someone Special." She surveyed the audience with a sugary smile. "My mother is *quite* special," went on Dahlia. "Why, only last night she was sewing together all these

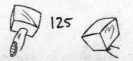

wonderful knitted squares for a quilt of love – for the poor, starving children in America."

America? mouthed Lewis to Jack, as Doris Dawkins got out her quilt of love – a garish mix of every shade of wool squares, sewn together.

"Yes," continued Dahlia with an emotional gulp, "my mother is *very* special. But she is *not* the Someone Special I have chosen to meet you today." There was a murmuring among the teachers and across the faces of the perfectly still children, hundreds of eyebrows shot up in polite surprise, like a well-organized troupe of trampolining caterpillars. Doris Dawkins also looked rather surprised.

"Oh no," moaned Jack, as Dahlia pulled out a piece of paper from her pocket – and then a little glass bottle half-filled with yellow liquid. "She wouldn't!"

Lewis leaped towards her, trying to grab it from her but Dahlia stepped back and Baz the ex-bully stepped forward to restrain Lewis.

She wagged her finger at him. "Should have joined on, Lewis! You should have joined on!"

she said. "Now it's too late for *you*," she dropped
some mead from the bottle on to her drawing.

"My Someone Special," she said to the
audience, "is much more special than my
mum!"

"Dahlia!" squawked Doris, dropping her
quilt of love.

"My Someone Special is special – because
she was made by *me!*" Dahlia blew on the damp
paper.

There was a moment of shocked silence and
then a commotion from the side of the stage.

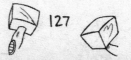

127

Then the stage lights suddenly went up to full beam and out, in a storm of marshmallows, danced Care-a-mite.

The screaming came from the teachers – and the grown-ups on stage. As the only ones not wearing friendship bracelets, it seemed they were not brainwashed by Dahlia. In Tauronia, Care-a-mite had been ghastly enough, thought Jack, but here in the real world she really looked quite scary, with her nasty smile and her finger-knitted hair and her weirdly fuzzy pink skin.

"Hello, everyone! I'm Care-a-mite and you're *live* on the Care-a-mite Show!" trilled Dahlia's creature. There was a moment of silence and then Dahlia shouted to her minions, "Cheer and clap, then, you idiots!"

Immediately a storm of wild applause, cheering and whooping engulfed the room and Care-a-mite stood on the stage, preening and smirking next to Dahlia, who was also preening and smirking.

"Thanks for joining me today," said Care-a-mite.

"Dahlia!" called out Miss Stretch. "I'm sorry – but this is a bit irregular!" She stepped nervously up to Care-a-mite, and tried to take charge. "Whoever you are, this is a wonderful costume and I'm sure you've gone to a lot of trouble, but we have to get on to announcements and. . ." Miss Stretch quailed as Care-a-mite turned to face her, the smile on her pink face becoming twisted and mean.

"Miss Stretch! So good you could make it! Now tell me . . . how much do you really *care* about these children?"

"I – I beg your pardon?" spluttered the head teacher, backing away and stumbling over. Aunt Thea caught her and steadied her.

"I mean – you *say* you care about them! But do you really? Do you? Do you? Open up to me! We all want you to open your heart, don't we, children?"

"Oh yes – we *do*!" chanted all the children. "Open your heart! Open your heart!"

Poor Miss Stretch opened and closed her mouth several times, like a shocked fish as

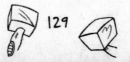

129

Care-a-mite put one marshmallow-filled hand up against her cheek.

Aunt Thea pulled Miss Stretch away from the Taur. "Lewis," she said. "Get behind me."

Lewis ran behind his aunt and found that she was holding a plastic carrier bag behind her back. He took it from her and looked inside – to find some paper and crayons and a twiggy bottle of Merrion's Mead. He gulped.

"Sorry I didn't believe you two, at first," muttered Aunt Thea. "Care-a-mite," she called, boldly cutting across the chanting children. "What are you doing in the Overworld?"

Care-a-mite spun around to stare at Aunt Thea. She did not look pleased to see her.

"I have been called out of Tauronia for a quest!" she said, her violet eyes glittering dangerously.

"Neither Jack nor Lewis even invited you *into* Tauronia, so I'm at a loss to know what you've been doing even *there*!" said Aunt Thea. All around her, grown-ups were gasping and murmuring and someone said, "Call the police."

"No need," called out Aunt Thea. "Everyone – please sit tight."

"I'll have you know that in Tauronia I am a celebrity!" snarled Care-a-mite. "And I have been called to the Overworld upon a quest to bring love and caring to all the children of this school . . . by my creator – Dahlia Dawkins."

"Really?" said Aunt Thea. "Well, I *don't* care. Let me open *my* heart. You don't belong here and Dahlia should never have drawn you and meaded you. The mead doesn't belong to her. She's a thief."

All the children gasped, with one breath, and put their hands to their mouths in shock.

Dahlia stepped up beside Care-a-mite, scarlet with rage. "How dare you!" she

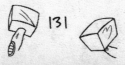

shrieked. "How dare you say I'm a thief?"

Aunt Thea whispered, "Get drawing now! We need help!" to Lewis. Then she looked back at Dahlia. "Your mother's a thief too," she added.

All the children gasped again. The teachers began to jostle each other and mutter anxiously.

"You'd better watch yourself, Miss Casterbridge!" warned Doris, stepping up beside her daughter. "I'll get my lawyer on to you!"

"Oh – I've already proved it," said Aunt Thea. She looked at her watch. "And the police should be arriving any minute now. You see, I finally worked out how you got into my house and stole the mead, Dahlia – you came through the ceiling, didn't you?"

All the children gasped again and Jack and Lewis joined in this time.

"Now just a minute!" huffed Doris.

"And you helped her," added Aunt Thea. "That's what all the DIY bashing and crashing was about on the first night you arrived. You were bashing through the walls between all the attics along our terrace of cottages, so you could send your daughter along and down through everyone's attic hatches, to steal things in the night."

"Lies! Lies!" shrieked Doris, while Dahlia put her hand in her pocket and looked meanly across at Care-a-mite, in a way which made Jack tremble.

"Of course, Dahlia never expected to find much more than the usual swag," went on Aunt Thea. "Until she found out about Tauronia and the magic mead. Then she searched through my cupboards and found it – tipped out a little from each bottle into a bottle of her own – and used it to brainwash you all." She pointed at the children, who all looked dazed and still very much brainwashed.

"Dahlia!" screeched Doris Dawkins, abruptly dropping her posh voice. "I thought you were nickin' the silver! Not some magic mead! You didn't tell me about no magic mead!"

Dahlia rolled her eyes. "Ah shaddup, you old trout," she said. "If I wanna nick magic mead and make stuff come to life, I'm gonna!"

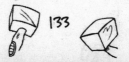

133

"You have no right to make monsters and put them in the real world, Dahlia," said Aunt Thea. "It's much too dangerous."

Dahlia glared at her. "This," she hissed, pointing to Care-a-mite, "is not a monster. . ." And she hauled another bit of paper out of her pocket, with a drawing of Care-a-mite on it, and then flipped it over and spilled mead from a little plastic bottle on a second drawing on the other side. She looked up with a nasty gleam in her eyes and a muggy draught of air swept around the hall, giving Jack even worse chills. "This," said Dahlia, "is a MONSTER!"

134

Chapter Twelve

Bashertaur

All the children, in perfect time and pitch, went "Eeeeeeek!" and put their hands over their eyes. They were well-behaved even when they were scared enough to wet their pants.

And they should be scared. On the stage, Care-a-mite was metamorphosing into something terrible. Both of her lovely violet eyes had suddenly bulged out and gone red around the edges, and dripping white fangs had descended from her sweet smile. Her chubby soft hands dropped the marshmallows and began to swell and warp and change into two huge grey lump-hammers. The finger-knitted hair and the roses fell off and a horned bony skull was revealed beneath them. The sequins

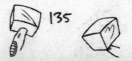

135

on the dress grew into rough orange scales. Grey claws burst straight through her ruby shoes. Now the teachers and the grown-ups on stage were screaming too.

"You fools!" bellowed Dahlia, her eyes flashing demonically. "I tried to give you a perfect world! To make everything NICE for you, but oh no, you didn't want it, did you? You had to have your OWN FREE WILL as well!"

"Take your bracelets off!" bellowed Jack, suddenly running to the front of the confused audience of brainwashed children. "Take them off! They're how Dahlia's keeping control of you!"

"Oh I wouldn't if I were you!" shrieked Dahlia, grinning. "Because Bashertaur here will only go after children who *don't* belong to my club! If you haven't got a friendship bracelet, you're not a friend of Dahlia's. And if you're not a mate – you're mash!"

"LEWIS!" yelled Aunt Thea, through all the noise. "Have you drawn it?"

"YES!" yelled back Lewis.

"Then quick! Outside to the playground."

There was a terrible
screech behind them as
Bashertaur grew another
foot in height and then
turned to look at
Lewis, foamy dribble
running off her
fangs and her red-
tinged eyes rolling
wildly. Aunt Thea
grabbed Lewis's
wrist and hauled
him off the stage.

"Nobody
move!" she
called to the rest
of the children,
who were now cowering in
their seats. "Don't follow us! Stay still!"

"OH NO YOU DON'T!" yelled Dahlia, as
Lewis and Aunt Thea reached Jack and Sarah
and the four of them ran for the emergency
exit. "STOP THEM! DO AS I SAY! STOP
THEM!"

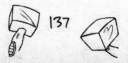

137

The children jumped out of their seats, but fear had made them confused. Some ran towards Dahlia's enemies and some ran away from them. Some just turned round and round in circles, squeaking.

There was a tremendous crash as Bashertaur jumped down off the stage. She was terrifying to look at and breathing so heavily that Jack could feel the hot blast of each breath on the back of his neck from right across the room, while they struggled to push down the emergency bar on the exit door. Aunt Thea gave it a thump and they all tumbled outside, followed by a straggle of confused brainwashed children and one or two shocked teachers, trying to decide whether to help or whether to crawl under a bench and suck their thumbs, in the hope that this was all a terrible dream.

Jack, Lewis, Sarah and Aunt Thea ran across the playground, feeling Bashertaur thundering along on the tarmac behind them. Bashertaur bellowed like an angry bull. "BASH THEM!" squealed Dahlia, running behind her monster. "Bash them flat on to the ground! Mash them like rotten apples! Pop their eyeballs out!" Bashertaur crashed her huge lump-hammer fists into the ground as she ran, driving holes into it and sending up clouds of pulverized tarmac. It felt like an earthquake.

Jack took Lewis and Sarah's hands as they ran. He glanced at them, sadness overtaking his fear. There was no escape. A bad Taur on the loose in the Overworld was the worst thing imaginable, and he and Lewis had no power over this one at all. They were all moments away from becoming an interesting Someone Special collage, spread across the playground.

Suddenly, ahead of them, in the high brick wall of the playground, a door was flung open and out of it strode Electrotaur in a shaft of golden light, followed by Slashermite . . . and then Wuffamite . . . and then Flowertaur.

"YESSS!" Lewis echoed, waving his freshly meaded picture in the air. "Now we're rockin'!"

"You've been *drawing?*" gasped Jack. "And *meading?*"

"Yep!" yelled Lewis. "While all that stuff was going on up on the stage. We needed extra

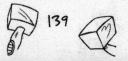

help. I made another portal from Tauronia. Aunt Thea brought mead."

Jack hauled Sarah and Lewis along as fast as they could go and they skidded around to the other side of Electrotaur, who stood tall, one strong arm held out in a warning to Bashertaur. Then Jack ran around behind Wuffamite. He yanked on his tail and pointed to Bashertaur. "BASHERTAUR made me do that!" he shouted as Wuffamite, fluffy and cuddly and doggy, suddenly doubled in size and began to slaver and howl like a rabid wolf . . . which he now was. He was Wolfataur and not to be messed with.

"Flowertaur! Take Bashertaur out!" yelled Lewis, and the pretty flower creature wriggled across the playground on his tendrilly feet, narrowed his assassin's eyes to work out the distance and angle, and began to fire poison-tipped thorns at their foe with great speed and accuracy. Most of them bounced off the thick leathery orange scales and then Bashertaur turned and crashed one huge hammer down. There was a brief squish and a grassy waft,

and when the hammer lifted up again poor Flowertaur was just a green and pink puddle.

"NO!" screamed Lewis. "NO!"

Bashertaur gave a big belly laugh and advanced upon them, bashing up more of the playground and grinning at Jack and Lewis – then her head turned and she looked at Slashermite, who was creeping in from her left, finger-blades out, snarling with fury. "Come to Bashy, Slashy!" growled Bashertaur and lifted one hammer-fist high above the little purple mite.

Lewis screamed again. "NO! Slashy! NO!"

But before Bashertaur's fist dropped, she gave a shriek of annoyance and spun around. Wolfataur had leaped on to her and was sinking his needle-sharp teeth into Bashertaur's shoulder. The stench from Wolfataur's breath made everyone go weak at the knees.

"Lewis! Jack! Up the tree! And take your friend!" shouted Aunt Thea, holding her nose and trying not to breathe in. "Hurry! I don't know how strong Bashertaur is. I don't know if they can hold her!"

Jack, Lewis and Sarah scrambled up the

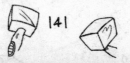

tree for the second time that day. As they reached the wide branch that grew out across the playground they had a bird's-eye view of Wolfataur fighting grimly with Bashertaur.

"FINISH HIM!" shrieked Dahlia, standing a few feet behind her monster. "FINISH ALL OF THEM!"

Bashertaur kept trying to bash Wolfataur off her shoulder, but having huge great lumphammers for hands made it very hard to dislodge him without smacking her own head. She was going slightly cross-eyed.

"IGNORE THE WOLF – GO FOR THE

SLASHING THING!" commanded Dahlia. "AND THE AUNTY! GET THEIR AUNTY!"

Aunt Thea had been pulling Slashermite towards the tree, but she froze behind Electrotaur as Bashertaur pounded closer. Bashertaur was now ignoring the razor-sharp teeth of Wolfataur, along with the stench of a hundred tins of cheap dog food left open in the sun. Electrotaur put out both hands and sent two jets of lightning directly at Bashertaur's chest.

Bashertaur stopped in her tracks, the electricity sending spasms through her big, nasty body. Wolfataur shot off her back and lay senseless on the ground. But Bashertaur didn't fall over, or stop straining to get to Slashermite and Aunt Thea, who were now frozen in their tracks on either side of Electrotaur, staring open-mouthed at the scene before them.

"Oh no!" moaned Jack, as he saw Dahlia pull out paper and crayons and mead from her pocket. "She's up to something."

"Yeah, well," said Lewis, beside him. "So am I!"

All of a sudden there were children running

into the playground behind Dahlia. Jack and Sarah gasped as a tidal wave of brainwashed juniors surged out of the school doors, ignoring the few teachers left who were trying to keep them inside. They were all holding up their left arms, as if they were pretending to be Superman, and as Jack stared, wondering what on earth they were doing, he saw that weird coloured lines seemed to be coming out of them.

Then he realized what was happening. The friendship bracelets were *growing* – shooting out long woolly creepers of finger-knitting at incredibly high speed. A vast sea of finger-knitting began to surge from the brainwashed pupils – a lurching, seething, alien growth tearing across the playground. It made straight for Aunt Thea and Slashermite, although it bent itself in a neat circle around Bashertaur and Dahlia.

Aunt Thea struggled as the wool reached her ankles and began to wrap itself tightly around her boots. Slashermite's finger-blades began to flash and whirr as he cut back the high-speed growth, but now it was up to Aunt Thea's waist and wrapping tightly around Slashermite's tail.

 144

It was up to Electrotaur's knees, but beginning to smoke and catch fire as the Taur's electrical current passed through it. Electrotaur ignored it and continued to blast non-stop lightning bolts at Bashertaur, just managing to hold her still as she strained to pound her enemies into the ground.

Sarah screamed. Down below her the finger-knitting creeper was shooting up the trunk of the oak tree towards them. "Weren't our hats meant to protect us?" she squeaked.

"Yes – against Dahlia's brainwashing," said Jack. "We didn't dream that *this* could happen. Lewis, we've got to think of something! FAST!" A bit of woolly creeper curled up in the air beneath him and darted for his dangling foot. Then it was round his ankle and yanking down so hard that Jack would have fallen if Sarah hadn't grabbed his jumper.

Lewis was frantically drawing a counter-attack.

"Come *on*, Lew!" shrieked Jack. "I can't hold on much longer. And Electrotaur is going to overload and cut out! And then Aunt Thea and Slashy are mashed potato! Aaaaaargh!" Now he was pulled right off the branch, with just one

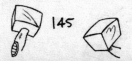

145

hand gripping on and Sarah desperately trying to tug him back.

As he dangled he could see the shapes of Aunt Thea and Slashermite – completely engulfed in multicoloured finger-knitting and hardly moving.

"LEEEWWWWWIIIISSSSS!" he cried, wondering if this would be his last ever word.

Lewis tipped mead on to the drawing he had spread out across the wide branch of the tree. "DONE!" he said.

Three seconds later there was complete silence.

Chapter Thirteen

Chilling Out

"Oh yes. I'm the daddy!" said Lewis. "That's the best one I've ever made."

Jack swung from the oak tree by one arm. Sarah held tightly on to his jumper that was now pulled up over his head. Below him there was no movement, although he could still feel the woolly creeper tight around his ankle. He kicked his legs and there was a crispy crackling noise. His ankle was free.

"Wooooaaah!" said Sarah, as Jack got back up on the branch and pulled the jumper off his head. "I never thought I'd ever say this to a year three – but you really are seriously cool, Lewis!"

"Not as cool as Floatingfrostataur!" said

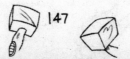

147

Lewis, waving his bit of meaded paper. On it was a drawing which look a bit like a swirly cloud with a strange blue face and snowflake-shaped eyes. Its mouth was pursed and blowing out a curly plume of silvery stuff. It had wide wings, and icicles for fingers and toes.

"Where is he?" breathed Jack, still astonished by the complete and utter silence around them.

"He's all over the playground," said Lewis. "Look!"

And indeed, Floatingfrostataur was billowing – a huge great cloud of Taur – right across the entire playground. The swirly cloud part of him had engulfed Shawley Junior and completely frozen it. A weird landscape of playground swathed in finger-knitting and brainwashed children pointing and gaping up at the sky was absolutely still below them. In the middle of it, on a round island of tarmac, stood Dahlia and Bashertaur. Bashertaur's face was contorted with fury and little icicles were beginning to form on her horns. Dahlia held her bottle of mead aloft and wore a look of intense, nasty delight. She had been watching

poor Aunt Thea and Slashermite disappearing under the wool. Electrotaur stood, swathed in finger-knitting to the waist, with his arms out straight and a bolt of lightning from each hand, frozen still in mid-air.

"What's he done to them?" said Jack, shivering. It was very cold and icicles were forming on the twigs and branches around them.

"Nothing – just frozen them into a stop. Not us, though, because we've got the caps on. Floatingfrostataur can't get you if you've got a cap on. Leccy and Slashy are going to need defrosting, but Aunt Thea should be OK."

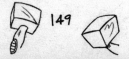

"Aunt Thea!" yelled Jack, and scrambled down the tree as fast as he could – which was pretty fast as everything was now covered in slippery frost.

He slipped and slid and staggered across to the mounds of wool and began to tear into them with his fingers. Lewis and Sarah arrived seconds later and joined in. Half a minute later Aunt Thea's head, still in its school cap, was free of the icy chamber of wool. She blinked several times and then said, "Well, *you* took your time!"

It didn't take long to free her completely and then they set to work undoing Slashermite. His little purple rhino horn emerged first, then his odd little face, frozen into a look of deep fright which made Lewis's heart clench. His poor Mite! He looked across at Dahlia. "Right!" he said. "I'm going to get her! If I smack her head now, it'll probably snap off!"

"Lewis – no!" said Aunt Thea. "We have to sort all this mess out – and fast." She checked her watch. "The police will be here at any time."

150

"The police?" echoed Jack.

"Yes – I called them this morning and tipped them off to come here for about midday. I planned to unmask Doris and Dahlia as thieves, and have them arrested. They are all *all right*, aren't they?" she added, looking around anxiously at the frozen children and teachers.

"Yeah – just frozen. Not dead or anything," said Lewis. "Except for poor Flowertaur." He dropped his eyes sadly.

"Did Dahlia and her mother really burgle all your neighbours?" asked Sarah.

"Yes – I found out how last night. They were clever . . . but not as clever as they thought. After I found out about the burglaries at number 1 and number 12, I remembered all the knocking and bashing noises that Doris and Dahlia had been making in the night. Remember I thought they were floorboarding their attic? Well – that made me start thinking. So I went up to my attic to check – and I was right. When you live in a terrace of cottages, the attics are all joined on to each other in a long row, with just one thin wall of bricks separating them. Our cottages are very

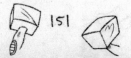

151

old and the bricks are really crumbly, so it was easy to do."

"What was easy to do?" asked Lewis, pulling bits of wool off Slashermite's frozen finger-blades.

"It was easy for them to take the bricks down and make a hole in all the walls, all the way along the attics. Then all they had to do was climb through and get into all the cottages through their attic doors in the ceilings. They were super quiet and neat and tidy, and knew exactly what to take. They are experts – both of them. I did some investigating and everywhere they've lived in the past three years, there have been neat, tidy, unsolved burglaries."

"Lewis. . ." gulped Jack, and Lewis jumped as he realized a face was looming over his shoulder. Floatingfrostataur was grinning at him and raising his frosty white eyebrows up and down, waiting for his creator to say thanks.

"You d-did brilliantly, F-Frosty!" said Lewis, through chattering teeth.

"Now w-what, though?" said Sarah, rubbing her chilly hands together. "Listen! I can hear sirens! How are we going to sort this mess out before the police get here? How will we ever explain it to them? The whole world will freak when this gets out!"

"We need a Sortitoutataur – at the double!" said Aunt Thea. "Something to get rid of all this mess and make everyone forget that it happened."

"OK," said Jack. "Why not?" He grabbed the paper and crayons and mead from Lewis and quickly scribbled a square with arms and legs and eyes and wrote Sortitoutataur, at top speed, along the top of it.

"What about Bashertaur – or Care-a-mite?" said Aunt Thea. "Are you going to let her back into Tauronia? Or will you . . . will you make her . . . un-be?"

Jack and Lewis looked at each other. "We can't make her un-be – only Dahlia can do that. Once she's back in Tauronia we can try to get Grippakillataur after her, or draw the custard chasm opening up under her," said Jack. "But we can't be sure she won't do something to get away, and anyway . . ." He shrugged. "I don't

like killing Taurs . . . not even Dahlia's."

"Well, just get her back down to Tauronia and we can decide her fate later," urged Aunt Thea. "Those sirens are getting very loud!"

Jack scribbled something else and then poured the mead. Three seconds later a rather sketchily drawn, square white Taur emerged from the door in the playground wall.

Sortitoutataur looked around at the mess, sighed, looked up to heaven and pursed his lips. "Really – I don't know *what* you'd do without me," he said in a voice remarkably like their mother's.

He clicked his swiftly drawn twiggy fingers and all the frozen Taurs sprung back to life and trooped, in an orderly line, back down through the doorway in the tree. Bashertaur shrank back down into Care-a-mite as she went, smiling sweetly. Wolfataur was now Wuffamite again and he, Slashermite and Electrotaur headed off back down to Tauronia, looking none the worse. Slashermite jiggled happily as he went. Then Flowertaur popped up suddenly from the puddle on the playground, looking most surprised. His petals quivered as he

trailed quickly along after Slashermite. He was probably in shock. In a whoosh of very cold wind, Floatingfrostataur gathered all his silvery cloudiness tightly to him and flew in behind them, giving them a friendly wave of his icicles and another cheery, chilly grin as he went. "He can live on the Tauronian snow fields," said Lewis. "He'll love it there. He'll only freeze things solid if I ask him to."

Next, all the frosty woolly creepers of finger-knitting unravelled, rolled themselves into neat balls of yarn and then tumbled over and over across the playground and into the doorway to Tauronia. Only one remained, winding itself around the tree. All that was left now were all the frozen children and teachers. Sortitoutataur clicked his fingers again and suddenly Dahlia and Doris Dawkins were defrosted and whacked unceremoniously against the tree, with the one single remaining finger-knitting creeper binding them tightly to it.

"You! You! I'll get you! You'll see!" bellowed Dahlia, trying to shake her fist. "I'll get my monster to rip your heads off! I'll get my

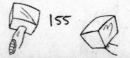

monster to turn you all inside out! Especially you, Sarah – you traitor!"

Sarah smiled. "Why, Dahlia. How can you be so negative and violent? You really should learn to play nicely."

"Oh go boil your backside!" bellowed Dahlia.

"Sideways!" added her mother.

"Now, now, ladies," said Jack, pocketing Dahlia's little glass bottle of stolen mead, which Sortitoutataur had flung into his hand.

"Quick, Sortitoutataur!" called Aunt Thea. "Wipe everyone's memory, except ours, of all magic mead stuff – and then unfreeze everything and pop back down to Tauronia, there's a good Taur!"

"Yeah – do that!" agreed Jack, and Sortitoutataur tutted and said, "Honestly – what would you do if I wasn't around to clear up after you?" He clicked his fingers one last time and then everything was back to normal. Well – fairly normal. A crowd of two hundred or so children stared at each other, dazed and wondering how on earth they had suddenly got out in the playground, all holding their arms up in the air like Superman. The teachers stared at each other too, wracking their brains to remember what it was they'd come out here for.

"A bit of a mess – that fire drill!" shouted Aunt Thea loudly and brightly, checking that the doorway to Tauronia was now gone. It was. The only odd thing about the playground now was the rather vacant-looking mother and daughter tied to an oak tree, but none of the teachers or children seemed to notice. "Perhaps we should all go back in now, and try it again another day!"

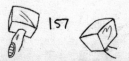

The teachers, even those who had been hiding under benches, sucking their thumbs, all nodded. Yes – a fire drill! That's what it was. A fire drill – and not a very good one. They would have to try harder next time. Everyone trooped back into school. Jack noticed that nobody had a friendship bracelet on any more.

Aunt Thea put her arms around her nephews and sighed with relief. "Right – that's enough drama for me for a lifetime!"

Then the blue flashing lights and the sirens arrived.

158

Chapter Fourteen

On the Fifth Hand

Once the police started investigating, loads and loads of evidence was found to incriminate Doris and Dahlia Dawkins. It turned out that Mr Dawkins wasn't in the Navy at all, but in Wormwood Scrubs, doing time for a bank job.

Aunt Thea showed the police all the broken attic walls and they found a whole roomful of booty upstairs in the Dawkins's house – including Sarah's little bead purse and a number of other nice things that Dahlia had nicked from all her devoted school friends. The Tauronian folder was also found and delivered back to Aunt Thea, who locked it in her bureau.

The burgling pair were committed to the

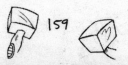

Mother and Daughter's Borstal, where all mother-and-daughter crime duos were sent to await trial.

"They'll go down for a good long time and no mistake," said the chief inspector as he shook Aunt Thea's hand. "Thank you, Miss Casterbridge. They might have gone on and on with their inter-generational crime spree for years before we caught them. That Dahlia always did so well at all the schools she went to. There's just something about a school monitor and Pupil of the Month that really throws a copper off the scent!"

That weekend, Aunt Thea and Jack and Lewis sat in the garden with the four remaining bottles of Merrion's Mead on the grass in front of them.

Jack and Lewis were solemn. This might well be the end of the road for Tauronia.

"On the one hand," said Aunt Thea, "we have all had lots of fun with this stuff, and more excitement than you can shake a stick at. . .'

Jack and Lewis smiled and nodded vigorously.

"But on the other hand," went on their aunt,

"we've brought hundreds of children to the brink of total mind control, upset the balance of both nature *and* two-ply yarn, seen a Taur pulped before our very eyes and very nearly allowed a nine-year-old evil criminal to bring the world to its knees."

Jack and Lewis picked at the grass. They could hardly argue with this.

"On the *other* hand," their aunt continued, "we love Electrotaur and Slashermite and wouldn't want to never see them again."

Jack and Lewis grinned and nodded even more vigorously.

"But on what I think is now my *fourth* hand," Aunt Thea wrinkled her brow, "every time we get them up we are running a terrible risk of ripping a hole in the fabric of reality and plunging the entire planet into a whole new dimension of unparalleled terror."

There was a silence for several seconds. Then Aunt Thea added, "Oh what the heck! Tauronia is *way* too much fun to give up on!"

"Yessss!" Jack and Lewis punched the air with delight.

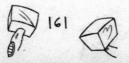

161

"Have you sorted out the Care-a-mite problem?"

Jack and Lewis nodded. "We will make all of *our* Taurs immune to her – and then we'll make an island full of Applauseataurs and Clappermites who aren't immune and who will always want to listen to her . . . and a pink boat full of marshmallows which floats over to it – and she'll just go straight there and never want to come back!"

"Brilliant . . . and nice, too," said Aunt Thea, smiling at them. "But not in a Dahlia way," she added hurriedly. "I'm impressed. But we are going to have to be far more careful in future,"

she warned, gathering the mead bottles up and carrying them back to the kitchen and the tall cupboard. "We've just had a nasty insight into how horribly bad this can all go if it falls into the wrong hands. Thank goodness we got the mead back from Dahlia. Nobody must ever, ever, *ever* find out about Merrion's Mead. Nobody but us. So, Jack, you know what you have to do."

Jack nodded solemnly. He went to the front door and then back to the kitchen. "She's coming," he said.

Outside, a small blue car drew up and a blonde-haired girl jumped out. "See you later, Mum," she called back to the driver. "Jack and Lewis's aunt said she'll drive me home after tea."

A few seconds later there was a knock at the door. Jack opened it and beckoned Sarah Adams inside quickly. Her hair was up in a ponytail and she was wearing jeans and trainers and a T-shirt – looking quite different to the neat and tidy girl in a school uniform that they had known before.

She grinned at Jack and waved at Lewis as he emerged from the kitchen.

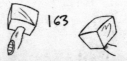

"You can stop looking so worried, both of you!" she laughed as she walked down the hallway. "I haven't told *anyone* anything! You said I mustn't and I haven't. But I can't *wait* to meet your Taurs again."

Jack grinned at her, but felt very guilty. He had invited Sarah to tea and told her she could meet one of their magical monsters again and she'd been excited all day at school. And she hadn't told anyone anything – he knew that. If she had, none of the girls she hung out with would believe her. They would think she was making stuff up and she would no longer be popular.

Jack and Lewis led Sarah out into the back garden where Aunt Thea was sitting on the grass again, with a tray of hot chocolate and buns. Slashermite was sitting next to her. Sarah gasped and put her hand to her mouth when she saw him again. She approached him carefully and then sat down on the other side of Aunt Thea, smiling nervously at him.

"Pleased to meet you again, um, Spike . . . um. . ."

"Slashermite," said Lewis. "He's my first ever monster creation. Um – no – I wouldn't try to shake hands. He'll have your fingers off."

Sarah withdrew her hand with a nervous cough and Slashermite just grinned and waved his finger-blades instead. "You – you were very brave last week, Slashermite," she said. "Bashertaur could have flattened you in a second but you still tried to fight her."

Slashermite beamed with delight and pride. There was a stomping noise and they looked up to see Electrotaur striding down the garden, sparks flying off the end of his tail and the tips of his lightning-shaped claws. Sarah gasped and then gave him a little wave. Electrotaur stood behind Slashermite and fixed the girl with his scary green glare.

"It's OK," said Jack. "He's just come to say hello. He's my first Taur too. Have some hot chocolate and we'll tell you all about it."

Sarah took a mug off the tray on the grass and listened with wide eyes as Jack and Lewis told her the whole story about Merrion's Mead and Electrotaur and Slashermite and all the other amazing creatures in Tauronia.

"Wow," she said, when at last they finished speaking. "That is just so amazing! No wonder you're always playing Tauronia games at school. But none of your friends know this is real?"

"Nope," said Jack. "Nobody would ever believe us."

"Not unless they'd seen it with their own eyes," said Aunt Thea. "And of course, it's important that nobody else does. Look what happened when Dahlia saw Electrotaur and Slashermite. That was the worst thing ever to happen."

"Thank goodness everyone's memories got wiped," said Sarah. "Nobody must know."

"No," sighed Aunt Thea. "Nobody. Not even you."

"But it's too late," said Sarah, puzzled. "I *do* know! And you didn't make Sortitoutataur wipe *my* memory, did you? I'm one of *you* now!"

"Yes. I think you certainly were one of us," said Aunt Thea. "Sortitoutataur never even questioned that. That's why he didn't wipe your memory. But he should have done really. It's just too dangerous for you to know about all this."

Sarah gulped. They were looking at her so solemnly. "What are you going to do?" she whispered, putting down her hot chocolate and looking around at them all.

"Oh, look!" said Jack. "Slashermite must really like you, Sarah. He's waving at you. . ."

"I do feel rather bad about this," muttered Aunt Thea, as they all trooped out to the Beetle and got in, Jack and Lewis in the back and Sarah in the front.

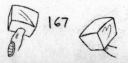

Sarah was smiling and looking a little dazed.

"You can't remember a thing, can you?" said Jack from the back seat.

"About what?" chirruped Sarah.

"You'll never even remember that you came here and met our friends and had tea, will you?" added Jack.

"Nope," said Sarah.

"When we're at school you'll still laugh at our stupid games and ride around on pretend horses and stuff like you always used to, won't you?"

"Of course. Why would I want to stop that? It's fun!"

As they drew up outside Sarah's house, Aunt Thea leaned over and opened the passenger door. Sarah turned around in her seat and said, "Well, thanks for letting me join in your Tauronia game. Maybe I can join in at school some time. You ought to have a girl in Tauronia once in a while. We can make up great monsters too, you know!"

Jack and Lewis shivered.

 168

"On the *fifth* hand," said Aunt Thea, driving off, "maybe we shouldn't have hypnotized her. I rather like her. Maybe we should get her back and . . . well. Maybe. One day."

Look out for more fantastic
Monster Maker adventures!

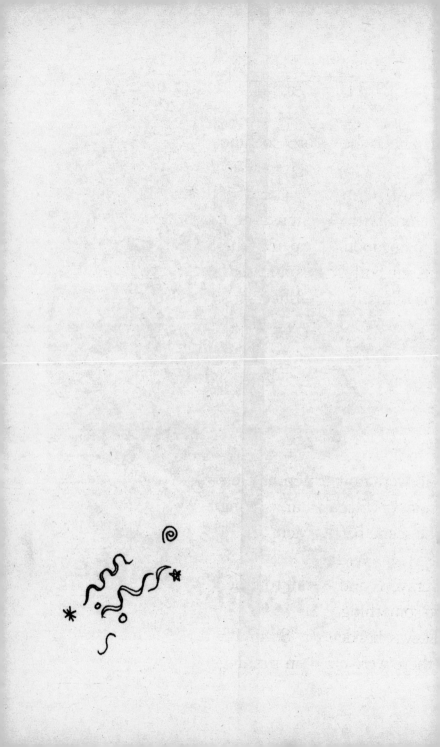